Faceless

By P.J. Verfall

Howling in the Dark 2024

"P.J. Verfall bursts onto the scene with old school splatter. This is a brutal, bloody, finely tuned gorefest that you won't want to miss!"-R.J. Benetti author of *The Slappening*

" It's brutal right out the gate!"- Carver Pike author of *Faces of Beth*

"Thought provoking and nasty as Hell. This was a wild, intense, and gripping ride through an intriguing, disturbed psyche." -No Remorse Reviews

"Like the twisted coupling of Henry Lee Lucas and Ottis Toole mixed with Jeffrey Dahmer and a massive dose of Splatterpunk! This book is vile and disgusting. If you like your horror on the hardcore side, you'll love Faceless."-Robert Essig author *Baby Fights*

"Disgustingly good! A well-written and in-depth shocker!" -Judith Sonnet, author of *Summer Never Ends*

Faceless

By PJ Verfall

Howling in the Dark Books 2024

Contact Howling in the Dark Books at

Holyrooster76 @ Gmail . com

Contents

Thanks to my beta readers, Tim Murr, John Foley, Steven Godfrey, Paul Synuria, Natasha Fedyszyn Zobym, and Alexa Poli-Scheigert

"Being like everybody is the same as being nobody."
—Rod Serling

"Sin, young man, is when you treat people like things.
Including yourself. That's what sin is."
—Terry Pratchett

"But there is genius in their hatred
there is enough genius in their hatred to kill you
to kill anybody"-Charles Bukowski

Chapter Zero

"YOU FUCKING LYING WHORE! NONE OF THIS WAS EVER MINE!"

BANG!

"Daddy! Please....stop!"

BANG!

pause

panting breath

longer pause

"Please!"

BANG!

...

Two figures sat in a bus terminal staring at the floor, trying to remember how to speak. Not really a bus terminal, nothing that grand and lofty, it was more a side room the bus company rented from the adjoining diner. A couple of chairs under a single bulb that thankfully didn't illuminate the grime on the walls. But this was all the bus terminal a town like this deserved or wanted. The man's bearded face looked resigned and sad, lines appearing where normally there were none, as much a product of the poor light as they were age or emotion. He leaned back against the wall, his t-shirt bulging in a way that attested to hard labor. The woman was much smaller than her companion, her face was pensive but even in this light it was too smooth to even suggest any future wrinkles.

"Sure, I can't talk you out of it?" He looked up as he asked.

She smiled wanly, "No, just like you couldn't the other times you tried. But you already knew that didn't you?"

He smiled back softly, "Yep, but you knew I had to ask at least once more before the bus got here."

She sighed, "Must be nice to just know things like you do."

He shook his head, "Sometimes it is, I guess. Half the time though, you just have to let things run their course no matter what you know. But at least I never get cheated at poker."

"Is that why you've been trying to talk me out of this? Because you know something?"

This brought a sigh, "Or maybe, just maybe, I could just not like it because I'm your brother and I'll miss you. Ever think of that? You're going where I can't protect you, hell, I can't even give you a hug if you've had a bad day."

They both sat in silence for a while. Not total silence, there was the banging and clattering from the diner behind them to intrude. The world refused to respect the little drama being played out in this side room, the world doesn't respect much at all. The noise coming through the closed door only managed to accentuate how cut off they were from the world in this little room.

Just two people and some hastily packed ancient and bulging suitcases. Boxes of escape that had probably not been used for several Presidential administrations; people didn't escape from here.

"You know he won't hurt you no more, right?"

She nodded, "I know that, I do, but seeing here will keep hurting me. Deep inside where it will hurt the most. Being stuck in this rinky-dink little town with everyone I went to high school with will hurt me too. You're happy here, and that's fine. I want you to be happy. But for me, it's like a jail where you just can't see the bars on the windows. Well, for good or for bad, when everything was over, for some reason this made me feel like I was looking at an open jail cell door all this time and just didn't know it. All I had to do was get the hell up and walk on through."

"I sure will miss you though Carol."

She laughed, it sounded a little forced, but it wasn't, she was just nervous. "You said that, you silly. It's not like I'm going to Mars, John. You can come visit when I have a place."

He smiled, "Me in a city? Might as well be on Mars."

They were interrupted by the large squealing Greyhound that pulled into the lot spewing smoke into the gray skies.

"Wish I knew how this was going to end," she said.

"Wish I could keep you home," he replied.

"I guess nobody gets what they want all the time,"

she replied softly before stepping out of the room. He got up to follow her just in time to see the great silver beast outside devour her.

Chapter 1

We wander through this life never needing more of the picture than a glance, our eyes darting over one face after another. A parade marches before us, a veritable stack of photos being rifled through, drifting past our memories. But how much of it can we say we retain for more than a moment? If you were asked, no, had it outright demanded of you to describe the convenience store clerk you bought Gatorade from two years ago, would you have a chance of succeeding? You had an actual human interaction with this person, but if forced at gunpoint at best you would come up with some generic description of every convenience store clerk you've run into from that day to now. Most likely, you still wouldn't be far wrong in your final description. Funny that.

On any street, at any time, you see a few pretty faces, and a few more that are notably ugly, but are any of them extraordinary enough to even register as a retained memory? Someone special enough they remained locked in your cerebral cortex for later examination? Or is it just, ho-hum, another day, another dollar? You live your life surrounded by a rotating mob that doesn't truly exist to you at all; in your line of sight one moment, gone forever the next.

Even the people you talk to briefly. Remove them from the room for long enough, you remember what you personally did in that moment, maybe, best case scenario. But maybe your real memory of their personality has just been completely tainted by your final memory of your side of the interaction. No worries, if you still need a person like that, you'll probably have no trouble finding another one any day now to fill that void.

So many people are more replaceable than they realize.

So many faces are so forgettable.

So many souls needn't have even bothered being born.

He scratched at his nude ass, smearing the red blood sprayed on it from earlier that had yet to dry. A decision needed to be made. Was there more fun to be had in this situation, or was it time for that last glorious crescendo before calling it a night? The young man on the floor in front of him moaned, but that was all he was able to do. All the struggles for his life and his future had ended quite some time ago. It had all dripped out of him onto the floor in a red river of surrender. That animal spark that will propel even the weakest to feats of strength seemed to have left him here, where he needed it most. But he knew that the dying form had one last party trick left before the electricity turned off completely, and in his judgment, it was about time for that curtain call.

He rolled the younger man, so he was face down, his ass in the air, pert and pale. He reached down to smear some blood over his engorged penis, slathering his member so it stood out like a crimson pole the maidens would happily dance around. Satisfied that all was ready, he reached back down for his hammer. You had to do this just right for the full ride. But then again, the naked man with the bloody cock had had lots of practice at getting it just so. He penetrated the pert ass again and thrust forward with a grunt before pulling back so just the tip remained inside fighting the mechanical clenching of the anus to remain in place. Satisfied he wouldn't come right there and then, he turned the remnants of a face where it lay on the floor, barely recognizable as human anymore, using the few remaining teeth to get a good grip where they poked through where the lips had been. Satisfied, he brought the plated metal hammer head down in a short and precise stroke.

As soon as the body began to violently twitch and jerk, the man plunged his cock up to the hilt. If you caught them in their death throes, the spasms were the best thing on earth as the colon and anus twitched like mad, all motor control short-circuited. All of the ride to get here was fun, but you wanted to end it with a benediction, not just something as simplistic as fun. It didn't matter the sex of the recipient of his attentions; they were all just meat tubes that existed for his satisfaction alone. None of them ever realized their real destiny when just the night before they had gone to bed with their pathetic little dreams of pathetic shit that they didn't even really care about themselves. None of them had a clue when they walked around saying "How you doing?" or tapping on their stupid apps. It was just another day in their minds, never mind what was coming down the road. Little did they ever suspect that since the moment their Mamma forced them out bloody into the open air, they were destined to die just as bloody, impaled on the turgid thrust of his masculinity

He lay there for a long while afterward, letting the explosion inside the embrace of death waft away from him like a dream that once was so vivid yet was gone in the morning. Letting that glorious feeling that exploded in his senses as the faceless tube experienced the Grande Morte in conjunction with his petite one float off into the ether that had birthed it all. Finally, he opened his eyes where he lay against the wall, taking a good account of what he'd done. He smiled; this guy must have been good at sports in school. Despite where Bentley had found him, the meat tube had lots of stamina to survive as long as he did. He'd stayed with Benny for hours of bloody, bloody fun and games. It had been a good night.

No rest for the wicked, if he wanted some of that meat he'd have to start breaking down the body before taint set in. He needed to cut off any still usable cuts of flesh while the body was still warm, the rest of the meat that he deemed unappetizing would go into acid. It varied from time to time, depending on what Bentley did to them, how much of the flesh was still good. Once denuded of their flank cuts and steaks, the bones were destined for a hydrogen peroxide bath and storage in the next room. Bentley's little hall of joy, his guide to past pleasures, his ossuary. If there was a spirit world, he could go there and commiserate with the others, feel their grief over what a poor idea it was to get into an SUV with Bentley.

He got up and scratched his belly before walking over to a toolbox that he had brought in just for this. Give him a table and a well-stocked toolbox and Bentley could take apart the world. The box he opened was all he needed to reduce a human body to bits and pieces.

To understand where we will be entering, we need an overview, a big picture that will make the little ones make sense, Picture the world from a slow-moving drone feed. First, we go down a country road near a large city, right in that netherworld where the creep of urbanization still hasn't defeated the woods and wilds and farmlands. The houses are sparsely placed here. It looks like a development was planned near the start of the winding shaded road but then never happened, the cul-de-sac road leading to nothing but weeds and grass. The further we go along the road, the longer the driveways become, the more trees there are, and the wider the houses are spaced. Soon enough it's nothing but woods and driveways with houses only visible from the road as unnatural colors seen through the trees.

The drone turns down one of the drives. It glides over the stone, precious little of it left, the driveway is overdue to be re-laid with gravel. After a while, sunlight shining brightly is visible up ahead through the gloom created by the trees above. The drone bursts into the light more suddenly than a child's first look at the outside world. Right in front of it is a house. It might have been a nice enough two-story house once. Now, the siding is faded, the paint peeled up a bit on the porch, the yard is overgrown to the point that it would take more than the average mower to return it to a lawn. The car parked in front of the garage is an anomaly, a nice, newer SUV. It gleams in the sunlight, contrasting starkly with its surroundings. The shining machine looks as if it's just visiting a poor relative and hopes no one sees it parked there.

We go around the house and fly through the inexplicably open back door. Normally it wouldn't be open, but this isn't a magic drone, so it needs ingress. The back door enters on to the kitchen. The walls of the kitchen used to be white, they're yellowish orange now with a thick coating of grease on everything. Dishes are stacked up and overflowing in the sink, and next to the sink layers of mold grow in coffee cups. Numerous plates are still laden with gray and green mounds of former food. At least a half dozen fly strips dangle from the ceiling; each of them black with the carcasses of insects. On some of the plates there are bones and rotting meat, producing squirming maggots that will one day grow up to fly, only to find one of those strips. In reality, the room needs even more strips, flies buzz and hover everywhere. There may be a trash can in the room, but by now it has overflowed so badly there is really only a mound of refuse piled in one corner. The flies are fat and lazy and well-fed, it's almost a shame their lives are so short, because between birth and fly strip it is the best fly life imaginable.

We continue. Next is what was once a dining room, dusty, stained walls, the family table, and chairs piled with newspapers and books. One more sharp turn brings us to the living room. Again, there are piles and piles of trash everywhere, the remains of fast food and takeout, usually still in their containers, flies have found this room as well. The walls and ceiling are speckled with tiny brown dots of fly shit, almost creating a soothing pattern. There are also beer cans and liquor bottles strewn around in various levels of fullness. Of course, some of them are filled to the brim, but drinking them would be a bad idea if you don't enjoy the taste of piss.

A TV blares away playing some kind of documentary, it is ignored by the occupant of the sole chair in the room that can be sat in as he taps on his laptop. He is nude, well-muscled, but with a bit of a gut spoiling the effect. It's like every ounce of fat in his body has settled in his middle. His brown hair is stringy and unwashed, of mid-length, just touching the top of his spine between his shoulder blades in the back. He doesn't have a beard so much as a salt-and-pepper two-day scruff. He is reading something on the laptop now, his other hand strays down to idly touch his penis, which swells instantly to a surprising length.

The man in the chair ignores the drone, which is pretty easy, metaphors are easy to ignore, especially if you're stroking your cock.

He finally notices his erection, his stroking of it before had just been absentminded fidgeting before that, like a bonobo in a zoo. Maybe he should go take care of that, especially since he had planned to go to the supermarket to get some more frozen dinners today. It wouldn't do to be walking up and down the aisles with monster wood waving at the house fraus looking for fresh veggies and weenies to roast. Especially since he was pretty sure his only clothes even remotely clean were cargo shorts, and they tented easily.

He pulled himself up from his chair and began to move down a hallway that led to some rooms that the drone metaphor missed. Considering one of them was the downstairs toilet, it was probably a blessing the drone came directly here. That is exactly the direction the man heads.

Until he hears tires on the driveway, a sound he had only heard any time recently in his memories.

"Son of a bitch!" he growled. He changed directions and headed for a set of stairs not far from the dining room. At the end of the cluttered hallway at the top of the landing he entered a room. Turning on a low-watt overhead bulb revealed that inside was an avalanche of clothing surrounding a large four-poster bed, each pile looking more precarious than the last. He quickly snatched a pair of shorts off the floor, and a quick scan gave him a guess for a t-shirt to toss on to complete his ensemble.

He had just pulled the shirt over his head when he heard a car door slam outside.

As he hurtled his way toward the front door, he could see the woman coming up the walkway through the curtains. She hadn't seen his shadow in the window, she was busy scanning the house. 20's, formally dressed, attractive, he wondered if the Jehovah's Witnesses were out today. Weird for them to just send one out by herself like that, a girl could get hurt.

He watched the tall brunette stride purposely up his overgrown walkway toward the house her natural curls bouncing with the force of each step. She was a pretty girl, looked strong too, probably had good stamina. She probably worked out at least four days a week to keep that trim form. She was wearing a suit jacket, but the arms looked full instead of hanging on her, and the way her calves flexed exposed by her skirt told him she was doing something for fitness. Either that or she was working on a farm. Her face didn't look right for a JW, or a farmer for that matter. Usually, Witnesses were young and looked drugged out on bliss when you saw one out in the great big world. Her, she looked like she'd just stepped in something disgusting, and then something more disgusting than the last repulsive step. That was worrisome, but she didn't look like a cop either, they had better clothes than that, so he tried to rope in his nerves.

He yanked the door open just as she was about to press the doorbell just for the look of shock on her face as she jerked away. "Who the fuck are you, and what the fuck do you want?" he growled.

"Bentley Thomas?" the woman asked.

"You serving something?"

"Ummm no, I'm...."

"Well, I'm Benny then. Now anyway, to my question, who the fuck are you and what the fuck do you want on my property? Care to fucking answer or do I slam the door and go back to what I was doing? Or better yet, call the cops to report a trespasser?"

"I'm Patricia O'Neill, with APS, I'm here to do a welfare check. Someone was concerned that you might be having problems," she waved her hand at the uncut grass, "with everything."

Benny snorted, "Oh really? So, which one of my nosy, pain in the ass neighbors turned their bitching about my grass into a fucking check to see if I'm compos mentis? I let the grass grow because it's better for the environment and my back, and if those pricks don't like it, they can kiss my hairy warted ass."

"I'm not at liberty to say...." Patricia began.

Bentley looked at her closely, he watched her eyes travel over him, probably looking for proof of personal injury to give her cause for further annoyance. When her eyes reached his cargo shorts, which were still tenting from just a moment ago, he noticed a small blush. He almost cracked up at that but fought it down. It was more delicious if they both had to pretend it wasn't happening. Bentley looked her up and down right back, but more critically, she was looking on the surface for madness, but she wouldn't find it there. He was trying to read her soul. If only he wasn't sure that she filed a schedule with her office in case one of these went bad. He'd love to show her around some, they could start with the bedroom and work from there. Bentley suspected she had a pretty scream.

Instead, he said, "Well, I am not at liberty to give a shit. We ain't got no homeowner's association just busybodies who need a fucking life. In lieu of me caring about their opine of my personal life, they can try fucking themselves."

"If I could just check inside to make sure you're all right," she tried.

"You may not. I make it to work, even if I work part-time. My car is paid for, the bills are paid on time, and I own my own property. Property you are currently trespassing on since I know you have neither warrant nor reason to ask for one. So, and I mean this in the nicest way possible, fuck all the way off, fuck off until you think you've fucked too far off, and then fuck even further off than that." And with that, the door slammed in her face.

Bentley watched her turn around and go back to her car in a huff. His hand drifted down automatically to his dick and began to stroke it through his shorts. By the time the car was turning around, he had his cock out and was rubbing vigorously. He closed his eyes, and let his favorite fantasy play out in his head. As he came in spurts against the wall, he was shocked by how his dream world had played out. This time when his mother came into his room she had a completely different face. A face that was currently making a right onto Tollhouse Road.

Patty slammed her hand into the steering wheel as the car picked up speed on the road. Could that have gone any worse? It was only a minor miracle she hadn't stuttered or said "Ummm" at him like a schoolgirl. She'd make it right, but it was still humiliating. She was getting in that house; it was just a matter of waiting until Benny was out for the day. Like he said, he went to work, and when he did, so would she.

Patty didn't give two God damns about his "welfare." Her justification for even being there was tenuous at best. One neighbor's complaint didn't show any kind of pattern of self-harm or neglect and she knew it. Thankfully, she was good at her job, and Andrew, her supervisor, trusted her to follow her nose on things. Today's failure was only a delay, she had dealt with people like that before. She knew how to get into places like that with occupants who were harder to work around than Bentley. Just not today, today she had choked like a newbie doing a training ride-along.

Why?

Well, that was easy enough, it was probably because she was positive that Bentley Thomas was a serial killer.

When two of her clients had vanished without a trace, she wrote it off to things that happened to the kind of people she was dealing with. One she had known had been using meth and the other was a boy known to have an abusive home life. Both had been dutifully investigated by her and the police, both had been written off as runaways. Meth heads have dealers they want to avoid, and your gay boys with abusive right-wing drunken fathers have every reason on earth to run for it. It was expected they'd turn up, either in a jail cell or in a morgue, but the only thing keeping the case open was the lack of a body to burn.

The boy was sad, really his only flaw in life was who he had as a father. It was a common enough tale of woe. The problem with giving it too much time in her head was that the job was sad by its nature. Patty had long ago run out of sadness. Sadness had been blown away in the flamethrower of abuse and neglect and filling out reports nobody would ever read. It seemed like most of the time these fuck ups thought you were their mom, and that they were being fucking clever by hiding their problems from you. So, in the midst of all of it, you would get some kid or more likely a woman who really did need your help, and all you could do was follow protocol and hope for the best while you wasted your day chasing after some other asshole trying to game the system. And then one day the kid or woman ended up in a morgue as often as not. Usually, because they were somehow saddled with one of the assholes who treated you like their mom.

It was how you ended up going from a bright-eyed college graduate thinking you could fix a damned thing on this shithole planet to where she was now. Fuck 'em all. Let fire burn the land before she cared for another of these dead-ended simpletons. She had gone past resignation to it, she was somewhere else now. Somewhere in the dark, with a monster that panted and growled all the time.

And fuck 'em all was why she had been following a client. The bitch had lied to her and lied to her repeatedly and Patty wanted to catch her in the act. There was how the woman appeared in public, the perception she wanted to create for the judge and her social worker. She told Patty that she was just a poor single mom working a fast-food job and supplementing with food stamps to just get by. But the bitch had money for heroin, and Patty had been at this job too long to not spot a junkie maintaining.

So, she wanted to bust the skank, and Patty had no trouble guessing how the woman was getting that money, she just wanted it on the record. If these fucking jackasses wanted to pretend Patty was their mom and they were getting one over, well, Patty would be their damned mom and look under all their beds for their stash. And more importantly, she'd hand out consequences after she caught them out. If for no other reason than to get the bitch's daughter into foster care before something happened to the girl that couldn't be fixed.

She parked her little piece of shit Ford Focus and waited. There were three cheap hotels right near where she was parked, all of them had an unadvertised hourly rate for the discerning whore who didn't want to get seat belt impressions on her ass or have to fuck in an alley. If her assumption about Audra was correct, she'd be seeing the lying bitch shortly. Patty had caught "angelic pure heart" clients with a little too much money to spend on an obvious habit out here before. Audra didn't strike her as smart enough to be different.

And sure enough, there the scrawny little liar was getting let out of an SUV. She was barely wearing anything, and still, her face looked like she'd been running, red cheeks that weren't coming from the hooker rouge she was wearing. Unfortunately, hanging out with whores while being rosy faced was no proof of whoring. Patty took a few pictures, and then she waited for something more convincing. She needed to catch the bitch hopping into a car. Bonus points if her friend Andy on the force just happened to be able to link the plates to a known John.

She didn't have to wait long. Within ten minutes a nice new SUV pulled up. Audra leaned in and a few words were exchanged. A moment later she got in and they drove off. Patty had pics of all of it. It wasn't absolute proof, but it should be enough.

It took three days to finally get a protective custody order on her daughter Katrina. The thing there was, Katrina had been taking care of herself for the previous three days with no sign of her mother since that night. As well as a nine-year-old can take care of herself that was. She practically rushed to go with Patty, thrilled to see a familiar face who could offer protection and, even better, food. Katrina cried and told Patty that Audra had never come home that night. Or any night since then.

The plates came back to one Bentley Thomas. No criminal record, but an outstanding notice from a neighbor calling in complaints about his house that were thinly veiled as concern for Bentley's well-being. On its own, it might not have been much, but Patty had asked around again starting by talking to the missing boy, William's friends. Asking if any of them had seen an SUV like in the description and photos. One of them, who had a secret he was keeping from his own family, mentioned he'd seen something like that at the park in the city where they sometimes went. Where quite a few men who had a secret went to meet boys like that, close to a nearby bar, but far enough away to provide plausible deniability for the owners.

She never told Andy anything about the plates she'd had him run. He knew leads sometimes turned out to be nothing and never asked.

Patty had wanted to meet Bentley Thomas on her own.

Well, now that that was over and handled, he just needed to get that entire encounter out of his system. It didn't help that he felt like he needed to wait a couple of days to really wipe the slate because he had to make sure the bitch wasn't watching his house. To a degree it didn't matter, Bentley had sensors and cameras over the entire property, she couldn't get close enough to know enough to be more than an irritation. One of the big secrets about his life was that he only worked his job to appear normal. When his family died Bentley's financial woes more or less vanished forever. Dad had been a real go-getter, he'd made quite a bit of himself, and quite a bit of money doing it. As the only surviving heir, well, Bentley had made out quite well. Bentley didn't have to do shit he didn't want to. That kind of money can buy you a hell of a security setup, especially if you personally monitor it instead of having a company do it.

She hadn't been on the road in front of his house all week. He had cameras his neighbors didn't know about along the road heading toward the nearest subdivision. That rat trap car of hers hadn't been within two miles of this place. It had taken too long to be sure, but Bentley finally felt she'd taken his fuck off to heart and he could feel free to get back to his life. Well, the most enjoyable part of his life, working and living like a slob were just facts of existence, everybody did that. The real fun was on a Friday night like tonight, off in the city where all the bright lights and lost souls were. He got in the Wagoneer and went to find some action.

Benny made sure he had plenty of fuel, as he wove through downtown and worked his way to the northeast part of the city. This was not a place he wanted to get stranded, even if he was just passing through. He knew he wouldn't be parking the thing and getting out, so he'd also grabbed snacks. Smoke drifted lazily around the cabin as he exhaled, even with the window cracked. It had cost him extra to get the ashtray in this thing, but he'd be damned if he was pigging up the Jeep. He loved this SUV, it was his, and his alone, and things like that were important to him. He didn't smoke all the time, only on special occasions. The tension building in him from that bitch social worker combined with anticipation warranted a Camel.

The streetlights appeared to be more spaced out in this part of town. The actual poles weren't, but at some point, they'd either burned out or been shot out by shadows looking to keep their secrets. Things that happened inside the boarded-up buildings that the world thought of as abandoned wanted no light to shine upon them. Nobody wanted to see that. Especially those secrets involving commerce, commerce that was never declared to the IRS or even to God at confession. There were two well-lit intersections in this neighborhood, he didn't want them. He wanted what was half a block from them. Obvious, easy to find, but dark enough to keep its mouth shut.

That's where the extra special good girls were. And Bentley wanted one of them.

As expected, there was a gaggle of the normal working girls at one of the normal spots. All of them made it obvious by what they were wearing why they were there. Hookers never looked that different year in and year out, they had to sell a product, so they had to cater to their clientele, and men were such simple creatures. If fishnet stockings and high heels made your dad rock hard it would probably do the same for you, no need to get experimental. The women who depended on the rock-hard dicks of others for sustenance had no intention of interfering with their meal tickets by changing the dress code. And rock-hard was how they wanted you, the sooner you were in and out, the sooner out of your car and on to the next one. Less of a chance of you taking your erectile dysfunction out on them.

Bentley cruised by slowly. They wouldn't do. They were talking to one another, socializing, they all knew each other. They'd be paying attention to who got into what car. He wanted a new girl, someone who hadn't done this long enough to fit into the whore clique. Someone who hadn't gotten another whore to put her wing over her yet. Maybe not baby-faced and virginal, but not an established face that would be missed either.

He saw her on the other side of the street. She was clearly working, standing there by the side of the street by herself frozen out of the circle of light on the corner. She was wearing a teddy, but instead of a skirt to show off her legs, she was wearing ultra-tight black yoga pants. The girl had probably put on what she had in her apartment that used to turn her boyfriend on, hoping it would work out here as well. A throwback to her old days, back when her boyfriends didn't leave money on the dresser, just bruises everywhere.

At the next light, Bentley made a U-turn and

headed back toward the girl. She was perfect, and he wanted to get back there before someone else spotted her, or worse, she had a change of heart about her new calling in life. He could already feel his dick swell in his jeans; she was going to be exactly right. And she would be exactly the thing to blot that Patty bitch out of his mind so he could at least jerk off in peace again.

He slowed his SUV and rolled down the passenger window. "You look lonely," he said with a surprisingly winning smile.

She gave him a sheepish nervous smile, "Yeah, yeah, I guess I am. I would love to go on a date tonight."

He turned up the smile, "So would I. Hop in and we can talk about it."

She timidly got in and he pulled off as she was buckling up.

In a quiet uncertain voice, she said as if she was reciting a script, "I get fifty for sex, twenty for head, we have to negotiate for anything else."

Bentley turned down a small alley that went through to the next major cross street that he knew of. As soon as the SUV slowed to a halt in the darkness created by the buildings looming on either side he said, "I don't think you've ever considered a price for what I want."

He punched her hard, right in the face. Her head rocked back and smacked into the glass and then lolled forward. Before she had a chance to recover, he flipped open the center console and pulled out a Ziplock bag with a rag and a bottle in it. As she was still trying to clear her head, he moved with practiced efficiency to open the bag, open the bottle and soak the rag.

Her eyes went wide, briefly able to focus enough on him to see what he was doing. Her hands began to fumble with her seat belt trying to get free, but she was still too dazed from the blow to even find the catch. She turned to look at him just in time to see him swarm over the console at her, rag in hand.

"No, no, no!" she managed to say in a terrified whisper before the rag clamped over her mouth. A few minutes after that, she was less talkative.

Chapter 2

Bentley leaned his hand against a wall, his body spent. He was only a little disappointed. She'd died on her own without him being able to choose the moment, her body just drained of any will to keep living. It was always such a letdown when they did that, it seemed impolite. He was just getting ready to give her the coup de grace when suddenly she was wracked with a shudder and let out a final gasping breath. He couldn't help himself once he saw what was happening; two more thrusts and he came. Too late, too late, his very important date had left without him. Still, earlier when he'd cut off her nose, even drugged, she'd screamed loud enough to inform the angels above, so it wasn't like she'd drifted gently into this good night. She'd given him memories that he could savor later, her at her most realistic and almost human. Almost. Even a dog will howl like a human baby if you take a set of pliers to its nose.

He took a moment to appreciate the body as it lay there stone still and face down, if you could even call it a face. No, that was the point, a drone didn't deserve a face, those were reserved for real people. And it was surely just another drone that was strapped to the custom-built table in front of him. He sighed, fun time was over, it was time to consider the cleanup. Around the area where her head had been turned into a solid mass of red from his ministrations, some of the gore had managed to drip onto the tiled floor below despite his efforts to minimize the mess. You never could keep it contained, he wondered sometimes why he bothered to try.

Carefully, he took a scalpel and carved a small piece of flesh out of the meaty part of her back and popped it in his mouth. Bentley appreciated her in a way that no man ever had as he chewed on the rubbery flesh, here in her final true form before disposal. She could not be unique when she was alive, but dead she made for a damned tasty treat. He was a native of the great white north, taking his blubber raw against cold and leaner days.

It must have taken a lot of energy out of her to scream the way she did when the nose came off. She could only manage a whimper when he removed her ears. When he gouged out the eyes, she must have become resigned somewhere inside to achieving the perfection he demanded of all of his playmates. Tonight, hadn't needed to be perfect really, it just had to blot that bitch Patty out of his head for a while. He needed to examine why that had happened when he had the time. Most of the time when he thought about fucking someone, he automatically removed the identifying parts of their face in his mind. It was how he would be seeing them in real life, especially once he got them here. Not her though, her face had not only remained intact, but it was superimposed right over his other consistent fantasy. Problematic.

For the moment, he really didn't have the time for self-therapy. Bodies don't break themselves down, and meat spoils quickly, especially if it's been frightened. On a plus note, this would stock the chest freezer pretty well once he had this spent flesh tube cut down to parts, and then he had the parts wrapped for freezing.

Patty was surprised following Bentley had been that easy. Maybe he just assumed that what he was doing was so outside the norm that no one would ever think its source would be a shiny new Jeep. To be fair a Ford Focus was a nondescript car and he was preoccupied, but still. She'd been able to pick him up at the end of his road, follow him all through town without being spotted, even able to make the turns with him when he went back to pick up the girl. It had all gone just like the movies, him the suspect and her the diligent detective following a consistent four car lengths behind. Now, still undetected, she was near the end of his drive with a set of binoculars watching the house.

No lights were on.

He hadn't bothered to turn any on when he'd carried the slumped girl into the place hours ago, and none had gone on since then. There was no doubt in her mind as to what he was after watching him drag the girl inside. She'd wanted to make him as he dumped the body, she wanted to see the cold flesh where he hid it, but he had made no more appearances all night. Some part of her needed to get close to the killer, to drink him in, but here she waited, and it wasn't happening. The house had just sat there empty as the tomb, and she had sat in among some trees a short walk from where her car was parked, her feet and shirt getting soaked with dew while her body responded by getting cramps in her legs.

In the distance over the tree line, she could see the first rays of dawn beginning to threaten. She'd have to leave. This was a quiet road, and her idea for a stakeout would work at night when nobody drove down here, but soon people would be getting up. She knew for a fact that one of them was a busybody. No, if she didn't want to find herself lying through her teeth to a cop, the time to go was now. She certainly couldn't say she thought she was on the trail of a serial killer without an ounce of hard proof. That's the kind of babble that gets you locked up for your own protection, especially in this day and age of castle laws.

The gravel along the road berm crunched under her sneakers as she made her way back to the car. Otherwise, the darkness was silent, even the animals of the nearby woods appeared to have called it a night. Tomorrow, work would be a misery to get through, but really, when wasn't it? Half the other social workers nursed drinking problems, so even on coffee and two hours of sleep, Patty would be one of the sharpest tools in the shed. She hadn't even intended to stake him out tonight, she had been just about ready to give up her nightly pursuit of the man when it all began to unfold in front of her. Patty had even just inserted the keys into the Focus, debating whether or not to just give up when she saw the Wagoneer turn off of his road. The night looked like the night for all her subsumed dreams and desires. All that excitement, all that promise, ending with nothing to show for it.

Her car just sat there in the distance as she walked, hunkered down in the dim light like an admission of failure. Ready to take her back to her apartment, away from her unrealized hopes and dreams. "Come with me kid, back to reality," it seemed to beckon. What in the hell had she really hoped to even achieve here? The guy was a serial killer, and she had no real evidence to prove it, she could know something deep down, but it meant nothing in the light of the coming dawn. Seeing him near some women who were missing wasn't evidence. It was unlikely to even get the cops out here, not without a body. It wasn't like she even wanted the cops to come out here, but knowing where the bodies were would have provided her some leverage for the next time she approached him. And she so wanted there to be a next time.

The guy had a job, she'd just have to wait until he was at work and find where he kept the corpses if he wasn't dumping them. He had to have left some evidence inside the house. She slid into the car seat, the overhead bulb making it look even dingier than it was. The Focus decided to give her a scare, taking a long moment before it finally turned over. Yes, she was leaving tonight, but she'd be back soon enough. She pulled her car out onto the road making a k turn to get back home. She'd be back.

Bentley was in his mother's room. Two rooms in the house were kept spotless, her's had been modified slightly to include a small stove so he didn't have to leave if he didn't want to. It was certainly large enough to include one. His mother had been an expensive decoration to his father, and as such, he allowed her things, so she'd be happy in her cage. In this case, it was the largest room in the house for her to use as a crafts room. It contained her little projects, none of which were more than time wasters, any obsession would be discarded at the moment she had tried enough to display any ability at it. It also contained a bed where she would sleep when his father snored, which was usually. Even with the time gone by the comforters still smelled faintly of rose petals. Benny added the camp stove later, the house stove was more for appearances and rarely got used. Bentley wanted the front rooms to stink as much as he could stand; the smell of dishes and socks hid potential other smells.

But not here, here was sacrosanct. Here was where

she had her life. Here was cleaned daily, he only even slept on top of the bed covers when he was lonely and wanted to smell her again, if only just a little. Putting in the dinette had only required moving some of her older projects. He washed the dishes as he used them in the tub in the bathroom that was connected. The other clean room was never touched, never opened, he couldn't bear to even look at it, that was Rickey's room.

He sat at her desk and ate his meal, some Sichuan long beans he'd made in the room, and a flank steak fresh off the grill. He mused that he needed to start putting dates on the Reynolds wrap he used to wrap his meat when he put it in the freezer, He couldn't remember for the life of him who this came from, but it was particularly delicious. If he knew he could remember to save it for special occasions.

Bentley idly watched video from his various cameras on fast forward on his laptop. He didn't expect to find anything of interest, but he liked to review the footage from each and every one of his little defenders. He fully understood the penalties his lifestyle could possibly create, and he had no damned intention of getting caught and suffering those penalties. Never be sloppy, never be stupid, never be arrogant. A little paranoia was a good thing, it meant he was still sharp. It was what separated his desires to cleanse the streets of drones from the mad killers who stalked the world sharing their lunacy. He had no illusion of special powers to thwart the police, his goals could only be achieved one careful trip into the world at a time.

As he reached the end of the tape video from yesterday, he only recognized neighbors driving in and out from a normal day here on the edge of the suburbs. At one point he watched as he pulled into his own driveway. Knowing what was lying in his car, and how that all ended up, the thought sent a flash of blood to his cock. Not distracting enough to need care, just enough for him to shift his cargo shorts.

Following him down the road was another vehicle. It parked down the road before it got to his drive and someone got out. He recognized the make immediately, the damned bitch social worker was driving one of those! He watched the figure walk down the road toward his drive before suddenly veering off into the trees. He didn't have the picture quality to prove it, but he had enough that he didn't need to convince himself any further. He knew who it was. It had to be the fuckin social worker stalking him.

She had now become a bigger problem than he thought she was going to be. The only plus he could see in all of this was that she must be doing this on her own time and not telling anyone. No way Adult Services would OK a fucking stake out like that. Even if it was an adventure on her own time, it still meant she had to suspect something, why in the hell else would she be here? She was a problem, but she was being a problem from out on a limb all by herself. She could be dealt with.

Fine, she wanted to know what happened behind these walls. She was going to learn it all if he had his way. It had to happen now; she'd forced his hand.

Bentley was almost at work. Traffic had been slow today, but really, he didn't mind, for a change. It gave him time to work over in his mind how he was going to lure that bitch in. He was about to get off the exit into downtown where his office was when his phone pinged. At a red light, he checked the message in his texts.

Well, well, well.

He put his phone on hands-free and made a call, "Hey Tim? Hold my calls for the morning, something's come up at the house and I have to be there to take care of it. Anderson? Reschedule for next week, I wanted to look at his file more closely anyway. Yeah, if it holds me up all day put together a list for me and I'll remote work tonight. Cool, thanks."

He made the next right, and then another so he was heading back the way he'd come. Showtime.

Patty worked her way through the woods at the back of the property, cursing under her breath as she went. She was not what she would call an outdoorsy person by nature and the going was harder than she'd anticipated. There were no trails, but what there was in abundance were sticker bushes and vines to trip over. At the moment she was soaked in sweat, and the hiking boots she'd bought two years ago in a fit of wanting to be an outdoorsy person and failing had begun to pinch. But she just couldn't see another way to do this. Trying to break into the house from the front just opened her up to too many opportunities for discovery. The breaking in part shouldn't be hard, the man was a slob, and out in the middle of nowhere, she wouldn't be surprised if there was a door just left unlocked. But out front, the way was wide open once you got past the trees by the road, some of it visible from the road itself. Just for safety, she'd parked some distance away, that was more than exposed enough. It might be harder like this, but there was a better chance to do it without anyone ever being the wiser to her being here at all.

Patty hadn't exactly been thrilled with getting up as early as she had. But, if she wanted time to really check the house, she needed to get in as soon as she was sure Bentley had gone to work. Thank God for coffee, she'd have never been able to get herself in motion that early otherwise. Of course, once she was able to see the house, she didn't need caffeine anymore. Despite her exhaustion from working her way through the woods and her early wake-up, her heart rate had accelerated dramatically. She could almost taste the anticipation on her lips as she sped up just a little.

She heard a vehicle door in the distance, followed

by a motor turning over. She froze in place, listening to the gravel crunch under the tires going down the driveway. Well, he hadn't called out of work today, so far, so good. Patty breathed a small sigh of relief before finding a large protruding piece of sandstone to sit on. She was close enough that she should wait a minute. Give him time to get to work, she didn't want to be in his living room when he realized he forgot something inside. It was a good opportunity to look over her gear for the excursion.

There wasn't much, a backpack containing a camera to document what she found, a gun, a knife, a Leatherman tool because you never knew, a flashlight, a headlamp, and a set of lock picks. She had bought and learned to use the lock picks a few years back for work reasons. A client had caused her to want to learn, in this particular case it was actually one of the good ones. The woman had finally pressed charges against her boyfriend, but every single thing she owned was in the guy's apartment. Because the cops had picked him up at work, they weren't there to let her get her things, and after that, for whatever reason, they were being recalcitrant about opening up the place every day after that. Patty was thankful to have those skills, never on the record, but they'd come in handy a few times since then, thank you YouTube tutorials.

Once she had gotten up and moving again, she hurried across the exposed space to the house itself. It turned out the lock picks weren't necessary to get in. One pull got the sliding glass door leading in from the porch open. Before she went inside, she couldn't help but note that the hot tub and the grill were both immaculately clean. Who knew, maybe the rain did more cleaning of Bentley's property than he did.

Inside the house though was a different story. Patty gagged immediately. The other door at the back of the house had led to the kitchen, which connected to the dining room she found herself in. The smell coming from there was abysmal, a revolting mixture of stagnant water, rotten food, and grease. Funny, even though she was past that all now, the welfare check would have yielded results if she could have gotten in the door.

The question was, where would a serial killer hide the evidence? Especially one living alone like this. The guy was a hoarder, she doubted it would be in any room his stuff occupied, he'd want to keep them separate, both in their own spaces in his mind uncorrupted by the other. All that crap might be garbage, but it was precious to him. In her view that left her with the garage and the basement, she wasn't looking forward to either. She figured the upstairs would be even more cluttered and less likely, he'd want the things he treasured most close by, close by and gore free. It would have been lovely if he'd killed the girl right here in the dining room, but in her experience, the concept of something as messy as blood getting all over their stuff would be horrifying to a guy like this. It was kind of weird to her that a hoarder would be doing this at all. Usually, someone who had that obsession was that way to the exclusion of everything else. Bentley would make an interesting case study just for his ability to hold two dysfunctions at the same time while maintaining a job. It almost made her doubt herself. Almost. But Patty didn't have a lot of time in this life for self-doubt, she had learned to trust her instincts, and those instincts had rarely let her down in the past.

She held her breath and went back to the side of the house with the kitchen. She'd spotted a side door there that could lead to the garage. It was a thicker door than something used for an interior, so it indicated the direction it went. As she walked across the dirty linoleum, picking her way carefully so as not to step in something revolting, she could already see there was stuff stacked and mounded in front of the door she wanted. It hadn't looked like anything had been moved in ages. Still, she wanted to do due diligence and check. Well, that was what she told herself loudly. Deep down she knew the real reason she wanted to check the garage; she didn't want to go down into the basement. Here, she felt like she still had some possibility of escape, down there in the dark...

The door opened begrudgingly. Inside she looked around in the dim light provided by the garage door windows. The garage was cluttered, but not nearly like the rest of the house. There was at least some sense of order to the place, and frankly, it wasn't any more cluttered than any man's normal workshop in the garage. There was a car under a tarp in the far bay, the nearby bay was mostly empty. She really didn't have time, but curiosity got the better of her. She wanted to see what kind of classic car a psychopath takes that good care of to leave it tarped over even inside a garage.

It turned out the type of car was a very nice looking 67 GTO.

As she dropped the tarp back over the car, she knew that she was out of excuses, it was time to check the basement.

It took more than a few moments to find it, moments spent trying to avoid filth and clutter that seemed to loom from all directions inside the house. The door she found was tucked in under the curved stairwell leading upstairs. At first, she had thought it was a closet and had dismissed it, only to be forced to come back to it later. Eventually, no other choice presented itself, and when she came back and opened the door a cool gust of musty wind hit her in the face. It seemed a little too much air for just a basement, but then again, she'd been active all day today with the hike and searching the house, she was probably a bit overheated.

Her hand fumbled on the wall until she flicked on the switch by the top of the stairs and peered down. To her surprise, down in the depths of the house was a finished basement, she could see the carpet and paneling from there. She had just assumed it would be dark and dank, Benny didn't seem like the guy to have a video game playroom for the kids. Carefully she made her way down the carpeted steps, all too aware that each step took her further away from easy escape. She had no idea why she was being this cautious, Patty was the only person in the place. She just needed to keep telling herself that. Patty mused that with her luck, she'd slip on the carpet and be lying there unconscious when he got home. All she wanted was to get some proof the guy was a serial killer, not to gift-wrap herself for him as his next victim.

Arriving on the ground, the basement was messy and dusty with things piled up, but you could just picture kids playing on the old tv, and the PlayStation set up down here. It was weird to see this after everything upstairs. A slice of Americana peering through the debris hinting at a normal life that got buried. There was a door leading out of this room, and since she wasn't finding what she needed in here, time to move on.

The next room was more what she had been expecting in the first place. There was a washer and dryer, a utility sink, and little else except for bare concrete and retaining walls. Unlike the rest of the house, it was surprisingly dust free down here though. Patty's hand fumbled a bit before she finally found the light switch. Once the room was lit by a sole dingy bulb she almost screamed with frustration. Again, there was nothing here! She was so positive as to what Bentley was but here yet again there wasn't an ounce of proof to back that certainty up!

Her eyes scanned the room quickly again as if daring the proof to have been there all along. But the room hadn't changed to fit her desires, again, there was just an empty concrete box and a washer and dryer. Nothing. Failure. A waste of time, and worse, she had committed who knew how many crimes on this wild goose chase. There could still be something upstairs, but it just didn't feel right. No, if he had been doing his killing in the house, he'd have done it down here somewhere.

Why was the inline for water not connected to the washer?

Why was it running toward the back wall?

Before she could even think about what she was doing, Patty darted across the concrete floor to look. She followed the hose line from where it came out of the wall for the washer, and along the far wall where a hose had been connected. The hose suddenly vanished into the wall under where she guessed the garage was, next to a box that had been left there. She moved the box to get a better look.

At first, she saw nothing, just a concrete wall like before. She stood there panting and frustrated beyond all measure, about to leave. This had been a waste of time from beginning to end, maybe the damned girl had somehow left on her own that night. Wait…. She froze, almost daring what she thought she saw to cease to exist. Out of the corner of her eye, she saw a gleam, turning her eyes she saw the small piece of brass embedded low on the wall. Getting on her hands and knees she could see it was a handle, not a large one, not something you'd notice at first glance. She grasped it and pulled.

There was no noise when a section of the wall about 5 feet high, and three feet wide pulled free as a door with greased hinges, smoothly and easily. Quickly she flashed her flashlight inside, this had to be it! Immediately after the wall, the way forward opened into a passageway! He'd actually built himself a secret lair, an honest-to-God lair. Patty almost giggled with relief; nobody builds a secret tunnel for good reasons; she hadn't lost her damned mind. She stood up quickly, dug through her bag for her camera, and took a picture in the dim light before stooping down through the entrance.

The passageway only went a few feet through what looked to be solid bedrock until it entered a room. The space was a combination of bedrock and painted-over cinderblocks from what she could see in the gloom of her own flashlight. It took Patty a moment to find it but at last, her hand fell on the light switch. Flicking it on she had to immediately shield her eyes for a moment to recover. The overhead lights were glaringly bright naked bulbs.

Once her eyes recovered, she couldn't help it, she gasped. The room was filled with every kind of tool imaginable to disassemble a human being with. Knives were in plenitude, axes hung from hooks on the wall, after that, it got more esoteric, whips, woodworking tools, a cheese grater, she was positive she spotted a scalpel roll, awls, screws sat on shelves or hung from the walls. The only area not adorned with something to injure was a sink in the corner. To her surprise, both the sink and all the tools were spotless and gleaming in the bright light. Even so, the smell of steel and oil filled the room, along with a scent that was almost, but not exactly the same as the metallic smell. She photographed everything, this was close to enough dirt on the guy, but close only counted in horseshoes and hand grenades, there was more to check.

While bizarre and damning, it wasn't exactly what she was looking for. She suspected that her real goal would be through the door ahead of her. She tried to ignore her shaking hand and turned the knob.

After the door swung open, she stood where she was for a long moment. Even in the dim light being put off from the tool room and her flashlight what she saw was enough. The hooks alone, meat hooks that ran along one wall, that would have been ample to freeze her in her place. As intimidating as they were though, it was the table that grabbed her attention the hardest. It had started off as some kind of operating table, but it had been modified heavily so a person could be moved and restrained in a variety of positions at will, without ever being able to defend themselves due to the straps that hung down everywhere.

Murder happened here, there was no doubt it in her mind. Screams of anguish had echoed off of these walls, dreams were remembered in a frenzy of pain, only to die birthing again on that table in a universe where they could never come true. Death left little traces of itself in this room. Even though the room had been scrubbed as well as the previous one, here there was only so much scrubbing could do, stains had appeared in spots, stains that attested to the purpose of the place. When a man uses the kind of tools the last room held, well, something like that would certainly get messy she mused, almost light-headed at the thought.

As Patty turned on the light so she could photograph this torture chamber, she was surprised to find there were still other doors leading from there. What on earth could this hidden lair still have to offer? It was all she could do to make herself not rush forward and see what was behind door number three. She had two doors to choose from exiting this room, she wanted to know it all, everything this place hid, but she needed to make a record of it as she went. She forced herself to take her time, to be methodical, to catalog what was in front of her with her camera, getting as many of the details as possible committed to pixels.

By the time she was ready to open the door to her left, her heart was thumping in her chest. What had started as almost eager anticipation had turned to fear of what could possibly lurk behind there after the organized torture chamber and rack of implements, she'd seen so far. Her hand shook more violently than before as it grasped the knob and turned.

Pulling the door open, she froze. Patty had never heard the word ossuary before. If she had, she might have had the word to perfectly describe what she was looking at right now. All the bones, stacked neatly and precisely in neat rows, filling her vision with death. Femurs with femurs, ulnas with ulnas, spines still intact stacked one on top of the other, and worst of all the row of skulls that leered down at her from their perch upon a high shelf.

Patty was stunned just by the magnitude of it. She could barely collect her thoughts enough to take it all in, let alone try to put a count to the number of dissected human remains in front of her. She tried to regain focus; she was here for a reason. Patty needed to document all of this and leave.

Her hand was fumbling about looking for a light switch when a voice spoke directly behind her, "So, how did my wellness check go? I mean, overall?"

Before she could scream a hand clamped down over her mouth.

Chapter 3

Patty didn't want to wake up. She never wanted to wake up really, when every day is shittier than the last it doesn't inspire you to be a go-getter who jumps out of bed ready for action. Her dreams were lovely places, they were very, very red as well. But something was different here, she felt like her eyes were being held shut; like something was forcing her to remain dormant. She was torn between giving into the bliss of her imagination or letting her ego fight against the outside influence.

A voice penetrated the darkness of her mind, "You're almost up. Good. I want to thank you. You presented me with a hell of a quandary this week, and here you are all strapped down and solving my problems for me. I wish they were all this easy."

It all came back to her in a rush, her eyes snapped open and then squinted closed as she was blinded by light directly above her. She moved instinctually to turn away from the voice and then realized she couldn't move at all; her head was held rigidly in place. She knew exactly where she was, and what kind of stains had soaked into what she was strapped to.

"Nooooooo," she managed to moan.

"No? I think yes, I mean you practically gift-wrapped yourself. You came here to die, some part of you must have known that, but you came anyway.

Clearly, that's more than a yes, it's a yes please," the man with his naked back turned chuckled. She looked at that back, it took her a moment to get her brain to work enough to place Benny. He looked stronger here, his voice more cultured and urbane, not the man she met at that door what seemed a lifetime ago already. This was a man who could charm a victim, who might even charm her, despite the frightening nudity he presented to her.

Patty fought to get her thoughts into some measure of coherency so she could use the only weapon she had here, her voice. Bentley was not helping her; he was holding up various instruments of pain as if he was examining them, mulling over their good points and bad. She knew what he was really doing, he was letting her see them. He was letting her agonize over what he was going to do to her before he began. He wanted her primed to scream before he even touched her.

"I really did think you were so much smarter than this. I even thought you might be special. More the fool me, I had nothing, but a feeling and I guess it was wrong. You really thought you'd be the hero and catch the mean old killer? Heroes only exist in books, the faceless masses don't produce heroes, the mob produces drones who panic just right, or drones just following orders so blindly they save the day almost by accident. But no heroes," he said as he set down a hooked knife and picked up a scalpel. "Did you actually think you'd stop me?"

"No, I never wanted to stop you," she managed to get out through the fear constricting her throat.

Bentley froze, his hand still holding the scalpel to the air. The room itself held its breath before he said, "If not to stop me, to blackmail me? Found out about my parent's loot and thought you had a way to ameliorate that pitiful social worker's salary of yours?"

"I hadn't even looked into your money," she said, her eyes wide as she watched the light glinting off the scalpel.

He whirled, his face a mixture of rage and confusion, or more correctly rage caused by his confusion, "Then what? What on earth could possess you to invade my house like this? Are you just that fucking stupid with curiosity?"

"I wanted to help you, but I needed some insurance you wouldn't just kill me before I approached you," she managed to whisper.

Bentley's expression locked in befuddlement; he couldn't possibly imagine that anyone would ever utter the words he had just heard. Slowly, as if fighting an internal struggle to get each syllable out, he demanded, "You....want....to help...me?"

"Yes!" she said with more energy than she'd had since she'd regained consciousness.

Bentley's expression had lost none of its shock as he continued, "Why...on earth?" He recovered himself and the expression was replaced with a disdainful sneer, "How on earth could you even help me?"

This was it; this was the big moment of truth she had been practicing in her head. She either got this just right, or she died here right now. But that was the nature of life, you had to bet the house to win big, and right now she had nothing to lose except her life.

"I made you for a serial killer. Me, a lowly social worker. I knew weeks ago. Now if I can do it, sooner rather than later the cops are going to do the same thing."

"So, how..." he waved the hand expansively that was holding the scalpel, making her wince.

"You're taking indiscriminately. Some hookers, some junkies, same areas most of the time. Despite what you think about them some of them still have close ties to family, people who will check up on them. They haven't burned all their bridges yet. You've managed to take some of them already, I've gone over the missing persons files, and I saw where the families might push for an investigation but haven't yet. Right now, I'm betting the cops don't care or haven't put two and two together yet, but they will. But me, I work in the system. I know who's out there, and roughly where, who won't be missed, which ones could die in their rooms and nobody would even notice until it started to smell, if they even have rooms. I can keep you safe," she said with such fervor, that despite himself Bentley was fascinated.

Finally, after considering what she had said for a long moment, and agreeing with a lot of it he asked the bigger question, "Why? I mean, you've been charged to protect these people, we should be natural enemies!"

"Why should I?"

"Why should you what?"

"Why in the hell should I keep protecting people who keep throwing themselves off of cliffs? I came from a nice family; I think I got into social work just to piss my dad off, to show I wasn't another boring greed-head or another boring future trophy wife. But once upon a time, I sincerely believed, I believed I could save them all. Well, guess what? As understaffed and under-financed as we are, I can't even save the ones who are worth saving. Even if I still had it in me to be savior, the ones who think they're getting over, or just don't care, those fuckers suck up a ton of resources," she told him.

"So just quit," he shrugged.

"You ever tell a mother and her three-year-old there were no more housing vouchers in the middle of winter? And at least two of the assholes who took the vouchers came from nice suburban families they could have run right home to if they promised to clean up? One of them, one of them got kicked out of his apartment for having parties...." she paused.

"I still fail to see...."

"The girl froze to death."

It hung there, like an accusation against the whole entire world for a long moment.

Patty broke the silence by saying, "You want to kill them, and I want to help. I'd kill them by myself if I could."

Bentley nodded before saying, "I do a lot more than just killing you know."

"God, I fucking hope so!"

He smiled, Bentley loved the fever in her voice instantly and found that he sincerely wanted this to work out. It was something he would have never considered yesterday, but now there was a bright new world unfolding right in front of his mind's eye. He wanted there to be someone else to fantasize about when he thought about simple sex, it could be her. He wanted another set of eyes on the work to prevent mistakes, that could be her as well. It could! She had impressed him more than she could realize, he could have a real help mate in this life after so many years of isolation as he did his work.

"Have you ever wanted to feel someone die at the moment they made you cum?" he said softly.

Something in Patty, some deep core of her morality had been crumbling during this whole experience. Before she had just wanted to kill as an abstract, as a way of avenging herself and others. But strapped here like this in the cornered rabbit position, she could see the attraction of the power position the dog had. Terror had burned away those constructs of right and wrong. She had stared death in the eyes, and unbelievably, she had intrigued it enough to buy herself more time. The closer she got to him, the more he felt like less of an attacker and the less she resembled the little do-gooder she had been coming out of college. The knowledge that she could die here tonight shoved that Patty's moral certainty into a pit that it could never come out of. The words he had just spoken did something primal to her, she felt heat building within her that had nothing to do with rage. The very thought... Vengeance at the entire world, but it could be more than that, they could subjugate it and make it pleasure them....

It was an entirely different Patty who said, "How about you not die and make me cum, and we can make others die when they make me cum. In fact, why don't we make each other cum right now?"

It had been so long since he'd had a healthy and willing partner he was almost confused by the concept. Bentley considered that she was just trying to save her own life and dismissed it. No, he could sense it, that there was a fury there that mirrored his own that he could harness to the great work.

It was a blissful union, even if he left her strapped to the table the entire time. She screamed loudly enough, but not in agony.

When they were done, he said, "I have so many wonderful things to teach you. We'll start with patience, you lie there like a good little girl, and I'll go make us some dinner. I promise you; it will be like nothing you've had before."

Detective Bill Hare sat at his desk staring at his computer, willing there to be some pattern floating on the screen where none existed. He spent some time every few nights going over the same reports, the same files, and still nothing even suggested anything that he could lock in on. It didn't change his mind, just because he wasn't seeing the sailboat there was still one in the picture, he just needed to look the right way.

"Will you give that crap up already?" Detective Burke, otherwise known as "the other Bill" and Hare's partner said from the desk next door.

"When I see the sailboat," he muttered flicking through his tabs on his computer.

"What in the fuck are you talking about?" Burke demanded.

"You know, they used to have these pictures, if you looked at them just right you could see a landscape, or a car, or a sailboat or something, but if you weren't looking right, it all looked like gibberish," Bill responded not looking up.

"Yeah, and I've seen enough modern art to know, sometimes it is just gibberish," Burke responded with a smirk.

"Yeah, yeah, you've said similar before. But I'm

telling you, there's something happening here," Bill replied.

"Dude, you have been on this job for how long and you ain't figured it out yet? Sometimes the garbage in this city just takes itself out. There doesn't have to be any rhyme or reason to it. They put themselves in dangerous situations, they ingest dangerous chemicals, sometimes, as bizarre as this seems, they straighten out and figure out what a shit hole this place is and go on to new lives and try to forget they ever existed here," Burke said for what seemed like the hundredth time.

"I know all that, do you think I'm a rookie? But man, there has been an uptick in MIAs out there. We got no body, nobody knows where they went, just poof, gone, way more than normal. Even the gutter trash is getting edgy. I'm telling you, there's a pattern somewhere if I just figure out how to look at it right."

"Well, in the meantime, I am going fucking home. I'll see you tomorrow and we can work on really real cases that we don't have to look at funny to see anything, because it was all just a junky with a hot dose of fentanyl that fell in the fucking river the whole time. Real-world stuff that you can figure out who done it by the way the wife shot him in the middle of his side girl and she's still standing there holding a .357," Burke grinned as he got up.

"Oh goody, something to look forward to then," Bill replied not looking up.

Was this it? Was this a chance to live again? Bentley's mind was a swirl of confusion as he seasoned the chops for the grill. He didn't question for a second whether Patty would stop him from killing, she didn't want him to stop, and he couldn't stop now. He had made his decision about humanity, it was only in this moment finally that someone had stepped away from the mindless, faceless flesh tube machine to deserve a face again in his eyes. She was the first person he'd met who had behaved as something more than a vent for his rage and his loins. She had already proven she was meant for more than to be disposed of the second he was finished with her. Hell, the ones he wanted were all disposable in the real world anyway, at least he was honest about what he really wanted from them. Unlike their bosses and their lovers who all tried to mold them into the perfect little drones without being obvious about it. Drones, who could just be discarded or replaced as needed. Even his victims knew it deep down, they were all replaceable. He took all that respectable facade away and left them what they were, a blank slate with moisture and body heat where he could relieve himself before he ended their miserable existence. He tasted their screams, unlike the cowards who would destroy them slowly, who only tasted their tears.

He couldn't relieve himself like that with Patty, she

was a human being.

The first he'd met since his mother died.

He was sixteen when he realized there was a difference between sex with a human and just depositing a load into a faceless girl. Except he didn't realize at the time what it meant, what the moment had taught him. You need life experience to understand a message that profound.

The night it started Bentley had been lying in bed when he heard the front door open. It didn't startle him at all, his father was out of town on business, his mother had been out with friends, and it was about time for them to call it a night. He sat there in the dark and listened to her move around the house, relieved that she had made it home all right. He wasn't a little kid that needed a babysitter, but it was still his mother, and he worried when she was late, especially if he knew she might be drinking.

She wasn't downstairs long. He heard her come up, heard the door to her and his father's room open. She was in there for a little while before he heard her come back down the hall, her feet brushing softly across the carpet. He heard her call through his door, "Bentley honey, you up?"

He called back, "Just woke up when I heard you come in." It was a lie, he had been waiting for her to come home, but he didn't want to seem needy.

A moment later Bentley's door opened, and his breath caught in his throat. His mother stood there silhouetted in the light from the hall. Except for her stockings and her garter, she was naked. He knew what he felt in that instant was wrong, but he felt it anyway. If the response was so natural, how wrong could it even be?

"Mom?"

She strode towards him, swaying from both alcohol and her desire to be sexy. She needn't have worried. With her blond hair just slightly rustled, her beautiful body, the garters, and stockings, she oozed sex to Bentley. At this moment, Bentley had forgotten completely what being a son felt like.

"All night I had to hear from my girlfriends about what a hot young man you've become, dear. How they might like to have you do some lawn work. I got a little jealous. Your Dad is gone for the next week, and I'll be blunt, I'm lonely. Even when he is home, he ignores me half the time. I need a man, and you need to become one."

His eyes were riveted to her breasts as she came closer, watching them sway ever so slightly with every swish of her hips.

"What do you mean?" he managed to gulp out.

She responded by yanking his blanket back, revealing his nude body. Her hand slid over his hard abs before going right to his cock, which was already stiff as a rock.

"I think you more than know what I mean already," she breathed with a smile.

He could smell the alcohol on her breath as she climbed onto him and took his virginity. Later he would consider how easily he had slid into her, how she must have been thinking about this the whole way home. His mother was a very, very attractive woman, she could have had her choice of any young man she wanted. Instead, she had chosen to spit in the face of drone morality, she not only chose him, but she had also WANTED him. It was a memory that pleased him.

The next morning, he expected her to remember what she had done with him. It would come slowly as the light filtered past the leftover alcohol in her system. When that realization dawned, he expected her to flee his bed shamefacedly, he expected to have to comfort her, to accept her apologies, and say it was fine and he was fine. He understood he would be ready to protect her from her false modesties and petty shames.

He learned that his mother was a real human being, with a real will of her own when he opened his eyes to see her leg and torso slung over his body smiling.

Not sure what he should do he said, "Hi Mom."

"Hi yourself, you want breakfast, or would you like to start with dessert?" she asked impishly as her hand stroked him to life.

The night before his dad came home, she looked over dinner at Bentley with a sad and serious face.

Finally, he couldn't take it any longer, "Mom, did I do something wrong?"

She smiled wanly, "Nothing at all baby, but you know, we can't keep doing this. Your Dad will be back soon, and he'd kill us both if he even suspected. Tonight's the last night for us."

He could only sit there looking at her. He was too stunned to even cry. It was like being given the keys to a sports car and hitting the curves with it. You think it will be yours forever, and now the owner wants it back. He had expected them to find a way to continue, this was more than just sex, it was more than any remaining relationship she had with his old man.

She patted his leg, "It's not right for you either, Hun. You need to go find a girl of your own. Trust me, in a few years it won't be nearly so hot to be doing me, age catches us all. You need to find some pretty young thing that will grow with you, that can be part of the rest of your life, not just your youth, not just fond memories like I hope you have of me."

Finally, he found his voice, "But Mom, maybe I don't want to. Maybe I feel like this is the best thing that's ever happened to me. You'll always be my mom, nothing can change that, but now, now you're the most important person in my life."

She smiled sadly at him, "That's today and today only feels like forever because you're young. And trust me, I don't mind the flattery, I love how young you make me feel, you make me feel alive again. I never thought I'd feel a cock that powerful in me again for the rest of my life. But even if I were to continue giving in to my own selfishness, the world holds a dim view of what we've been doing. And before you say you don't care, like it or not baby, it's the only world we have to live in. We've pulled one over on it, but it was always going to be temporary."

His mind raced, knowing someone was right didn't stop you from trying to find the world they were wrong in. Sometimes we even find it, that magical version of the universe where we can still have what we want. Some part of him died a little inside when he couldn't dig to where it existed. He knew that tomorrow when his dad got back, he'd go back to being a son, and she'd go back to being a mother, and all that they would have of their time together as lovers would be memories.

She got up and took the dishes away while he fumed. He could hear her loading the dishwasher in the distance. Part of him wanted to scream, "Why did you even show me this world if you were just going to close the door? Wouldn't I have been better off never knowing it existed so I could never miss what I didn't know about?" Part of him knew he would be glad for the time they'd had at some later date. At least his first time was with someone who was willing to give him enough chances to get it just right. He wasn't so much of a child that he didn't believe her when she suggested there would be other girls. He was also not so foolish to not know that you always remember your first. And his had been more special and unique than most.

He felt her come up behind him. She draped her arms over his front, leaning down until her face was next to his. She felt him rub at the front of his pants. "Of course, we still have tonight. And there's a couple of rooms left in the house we haven't done anything in yet."

When his father came back, Bentley knew it was over. If he hadn't known it when his mom put on her best happy housewife routine when his father walked in the door, he had certainly known it when he could hear them rutting through the wall. The hope he'd been holding onto died as he lay on his bed listening. He couldn't help but chuckle, his father probably felt like he was really giving it to her good, but Bentley knew better. He had heard the real moans; he had heard passion from the woman. What his father was receiving was a skilled acting performance.

You'd only know the difference if you really had given it to her good.

Life returned to whatever passed for normal for the next two months. Bentley had even started dating a girl from class, he had confidence he hadn't before and just asked her out. And Laura was fine, even if that was all she could be to Bentley, fine. She was a girl he could stick his dick into until he got bored with her, or until he went away to college. He could fake emotions every bit as well as Mom could.

Normal got a dent in it when a month and a half later his mom announced that she was pregnant. His father was thrilled, he'd been on her to have another kid for years, and she'd always put him off. She said she must have screwed up her cycle the month Dad had gone away on his trip. Or more likely, she had just given up on sex by that point and hadn't bothered taking them.

His father was elated.

Bentley smirked in private, raising another man's child was nothing to get so excited about. But let the man with the money and the connections to make the kid's life go easy have his moment. Bentley knew whose child she was carrying, and it wasn't Dad's. And when they brought little Ricky home, he had no doubt at all.

His Dad had even said, "Kid looks just like you did when you were born, guess me and your mom have a formula, huh?"

Bentley had never had the chance to make love to a real person since then. Drones with pretty faces they didn't deserve had come and then gone on to their boring little lives with someone who could fake it a little better. But Patty…. Patty was different, she was real.

Bentley had released her from the table for dinner, but she couldn't help but take note that he locked the door behind him. That was fine, now that it looked like she might live through this she had no desire to leave. She WANTED this. This was her angry, raging dreams made flesh, a world where this was possible, where release from all the pent-up everything was permissible, for no other reason than Bentley made it so. And if he could make it that way for himself, maybe he could expand the world he'd built to allow her in.

She was impressed by the tray he brought down, not least of all because it, and the plates on it gleamed. The man she had been told off by just a few days ago vanished in the glare of this new reality. She had been through much of the house, and nothing she had seen suggested this as even a remote possibility. He removed lids to reveal potatoes, beans, and meat, not something that would first catch one's eye as being haute cuisine to be sure. But she could see the beans had been spiced, the mashed potatoes slathered with thick gravy, and the meat sent off waves of aromas, suggesting a complicated marinade.

"Smells delicious, and you'd never believe it, but being strapped to a table for that long creates an appetite," she quipped.

Patty had no way of knowing it, his facial

expression didn't change at all, but she'd impressed Bentley with that. To be telling jokes...after everything that happened to her...

"Well, I like to eat well," he said demurely by way of a reply.

"I'm surprised, judging by what I saw upstairs...."

He chuckled at that, "That? That's all window dressing. I'm surprised you haven't figured that out yet."

She was a bit taken aback, "What do you mean, it's a mess up there, window dressing for what?"

"That mess is well orchestrated for the eyes of others. Although I have learned to live with it, it took some getting used to. If there are bad smells on the wind for some reason? Well, I'm a known slob. Police don't like to deal with shut-ins and hoarders either, it grosses them out. They'd have to have a serious concrete suspicion to even want to start searching the place. It speaks to your determination that you did," he explained patiently.

She smiled, "But me, I knew you were something special. I just wanted to prove it to myself before I approached you."

"And evidence might prevent your sudden disappearance if I didn't prove tractable to a partnership," he said the unspoken part out loud for her.

She just nodded, "And if you were me, and you

wanted to get into something like this that bad, wouldn't you have tried the same thing?"

He chuckled again, "I might have at that. No, I can't say I blame you."

They ate in silence for a while, the only sound was their knives and forks on their plates. Both masticated quietly, so neither could hear the other chew. The dinner was going well, a meal between two sophisticated people with common goals, Patty began to have hope.

But there was just one question she had to ask.

"Who was this?"

He looked slightly surprised, his eyes widening a little, but in a moment his calm demeanor returned, "Don't you mean what is this?"

She shook her head, "No, no I don't think so. It's obviously not chicken, and it's too pale to be steak. It feels too tender and tastes too good to be a cut of pork this dark. So, that leaves only so many options now, doesn't it? So, who are we eating tonight."

His face was still for a moment, before it erupted into an approving laugh, "And are you enjoying your meal?"

"Quite a bit, I was just wondering if we could give a face to the food."

He barked with laughter, "A face to the food! Good one! As far as the face, you'll learn, faces don't matter. Still, sorry to say, I just had some meat thawed from the freezer for myself. I wasn't expecting to entertain, so it isn't anything I'd marked. Probably best not to do that anyway, the freezer is in the main house. Why make things obvious?"

"That makes sense," she said, sounding disappointed.

She pointed to the other door she had noticed earlier, "What's in there?"

"A project, I'm not even sure if I'm going to get to it," he answered.

She nodded. A moment later she asked the big question, "So, what now? Do I just go home, and you call? What happens now?"

"I thought you'd never ask. This next bit is totally participatory on your part, call it an audition for your role as a real human being. You said you know them and know which ones the world will never miss. Well, we're fucking one tonight, so pick a nice boy you're willing to do just what I say with."

Chapter 4

Bentley was heartily impressed; already Patty was expanding his world. As he watched the aged and soot-stained buildings pass he realized he didn't know this part of town at all. While he was indiscriminate about which sex he took to the basement, they were all the same to him, Patty knew more about where the disposable boys were than Bentley did. At least, this particular boy, but if this one was going to be found here, Bentley was sure there would be plenty more nearby. The day was bearing fruit already without anyone even getting in the SUV. If he had to kill her now, he'd still have new hunting grounds tomorrow.

"Slow down a bit, I think that's him on the corner by himself," she hissed urgently. As they got closer, she added, "It is, pull over and let's get out."

"But usually I..."

She smiled at him warmly, "You have help baby. We talked about this, they don't all have to be a struggle. He'll come along like a good little boy, wait and see."

Later he thought it was funny, it never so much as occurred to him that this could be a ruse and she was trying to get help for herself. He just dutifully pulled the SUV over and turned it off.

She leaned over and kissed him on the cheek, "I'll be right back with the entertainment portion of the evening."

Before Bentley could even respond, her door was open, and Patty was getting out.

Patty walked with brisk, business-like strides towards the solitary figure leaning against the street pole. The posture said nonchalant, waiting for somebody, in a way he probably was.

As soon as the figure saw her his hands went up, "Woah, Miss O'Neill! Fancy seeing you here."

"Just where I knew I'd find you," she said, her voice flat.

The young man couldn't have been more than 21, but his face looked like it was heading toward old age prematurely. Even surprised by the sight of her, it still looked tired and worn like sleep was only an occasional visitor in his life. This was a face that had seen too much to retain any youthful gleam, and too little solid food to retain any baby fat. He tried a look of innocence like he always did when he had to deal with the social worker he'd known since he was fifteen. And like always, his face betrayed the real him underneath.

"I think I'm outside your official capacity now, huh? Me being all adult and grown up and all kind of frees me. So, with that out of the way, to what do I owe this pleasure?" He decided to try a different angle.

She actually smiled, something he'd rarely if ever seen her do before, it looked sexy. "Funny you should mention pleasure. I know why you're out here Eddy, your sixteen-year-old ex-boyfriend told me all about it once his parents took him back in."

"Hey, I didn't...."

She interrupted his upcoming fuselage of lies, "I don't care if you did or didn't or what was or wasn't. Not right now. But I know why you're out here. And knowing why you're out here, I'll be blunt, how would you like to fuck and get fucked tonight?"

Eddy's entire face froze for a second. Finally, he recovered enough to laugh, "I always knew you were hipper than you let on Miss O'Neill, an ass like that needs to get pounded, am I right?"

"He fucks you; you fuck me at the same time. I already know you need cash; you always do. How much to make a night of it back at his place?" she smiled. It wasn't the face he had known for years; it was a dirty, wanton smile; it wasn't for Eddy, but Eddy didn't need to know that. All he had to do was think about fucking his former social worker.

He grinned, eyeing her up, already picturing her naked. Eddy only did chicks for money, either upfront or because he needed a place to crash, it wasn't his preference. But with the woman who stood before him, that was going to be different. There was a power shift presented by the idea of fucking his surrogate mommy that he couldn't help but relish.

"What's your boyfriend look like?"

"He's cute. Sort of your flip side Eddy. Prefers girls, but doesn't discriminate either, rugged. He knows what

I like and wants me to have it. So, what's the word, sweetie? You wanna go back to his place and fuck or stay out here all night hoping for a quicky?" Patty made a point of licking her upper lip after she said it, it was cliché, but cliches in sex exist for a reason. Nobody went broke making push-up bras or lace panties for a living.

If Eddy's grin had gotten any wider the top of his head would have fallen back like it was on a hinge. "Hundred bucks, cash in hand or I don't spread these sweet cheeks."

"He's got the money, so why don't you hop in and get to know him a bit? I mean, you already know me, just not as well as you're going to," she said before she turned and began to sashay back to the Jeep.

"Well, all right then!" Eddy slapped his hands and followed her.

She got into the back seat smoothly and gracefully and let Eddy have the front. Rear passengers tend to be more nervous, tend to feel cut off from what's happening, confined outside of the group dynamic. They wanted Eddy to feel comfortable, like he was in charge to some degree. They'd need him to be chill when they got to the house.

"Hey man, name's Eddy," he thrust his hand out in Bentley's general direction.

Bentley offered him a light smile and his hand, "Bentley."

"Business out of the way first, I told her, 100 bucks

for the both of you. Cheap at twice the price," Eddy said.

Bentley sat up and brought out his wallet. He waved a few bills toward Eddy, "50 now, 50 when my cock is spent."

The money vanished like magic into the depths of Eddy's clothes. As Eddy buckled himself in Bentley, put the SUV in gear and pulled away from the curb.

Eddy had a thought, "Bentley like the car or the author?"

"There's an author?" Bentley asked as he gave the vehicle gas, speeding them on their way.

"Yeah, he writes horror and stuff, first name is Bentley, can't remember his last name off the top of my head," Eddy said still smiling. Patty wished he'd stop smiling so much, or brush more often if he insisted on it.

"Naw, I don't read horror, or watch it really. Just doesn't do much for me," Bentley replied.

Eddy had chattered the entire time they drove and both Patty and Bentley were OK letting him. They could tune him out and it showed comfort with the situation on his part. Maybe it was a nervous tick he didn't even know he had, more likely he wanted them to like him at some deep-down level he didn't recognize in himself, or maybe there were more obvious reasons than they realized.

They were taking him to their house, which meant

he was getting paid for more than fucking tonight. They didn't know it, but he was getting paid to scout the place for a later visit with friends who could carry a lot of valuables, so maybe he just chattered to appear harmless. He could never believe that people were dumb enough to take a hooker home to their house, but he stayed high a lot longer when they did.

When they pulled up to the house, Eddy couldn't help himself but say, "Not much for gardening, huh?"

Bentley chuckled, "I keep some parts of the house clean as a whistle. But honestly, until recently I was single, and when you're single..."

Eddy raised his hands, "No worries, I get you. Out hustling, no time to play housewife."

"Exactly," Bentley grinned. They had had a moment there, bonded.

Bentley and Patty had straightened parts of the house a little before they went out, Patty had insisted. With all the lights on, the house would still look like a hoarder lived there. If they were bringing people in fully conscious, they didn't want them to balk on the doorstep. And if they were bringing them in normally it cut down on the fun if Bentley hurt them bringing them through the house by ramming them into something. If the living room looked generally tidy, well, you couldn't see much else by the table lamp that was hooked up to the switch.

"So where do we go from here?" Eddy asked as he

tried to scout as much of the house as he could from the dim light of the living room. His nose twitched at the smell a bit, but he figured he had no room to talk, his landlady would agree with that.

Patty ran her finger along his ear, "We've got a playroom down in the basement, wait until you see the table."

"Table?"

Bentley called back from where he was leading them deeper into the house towards the basement door, "I had it specially built, it's posable."

Patty got Eddy's attention by reaching around to the front of his pants and roughly stroking the lump she found. "If you've got the stamina baby, it can hold us any way we want to move."

Bentley went down the steps, Eddy followed letting out a, "Don't worry baby, I got plenty of stamina, I take vitamins."

"Good boy," she breathed.

The table was in the room with the washer and dryer now. Bentley had moved it out here, agreeing with her plan to use a cooperative victim, one who would definitely balk if they saw the tool room. She was thrilled he had agreed to try it her way. Patty couldn't say why she felt this way, she had no way to articulate it, but at some point, they had become partners in this. It had never been spoken, Bentley had never even directly implied it, but she knew it anyway. He'd already put in some work to go along with her plan for getting Eddy. If he had some special initiation that he had thought up just for her, she was willing to go where it took her. Both were like kids on a first date, each desperate to make a pleasing impression on the other.

Eddy was staring at the table in obvious admiration, "Shame you didn't put it in the family room, more cozy, but man, that thing is awesome."

"You know how hard it is to get lube out of carpet?" Bentley asked.

"Speaking of which...." Patty said in a breathy voice behind them.

She was already half undressed when the men turned to look at her. Eddy greeted the sight of her breasts with a huge grin. They were large and firm, the kind of thing a little kid would love to latch his lips onto for breakfast. As slowly and as sexily as she could manage, she kept shedding the rest of her garments. She slunk up to Eddy and grabbed the zipper on his jeans, yanking it down slowly.

"Now, don't you boys feel overdressed?"

Eddy wasted no time, taking his light jacket off and putting it on the washer, followed by his t-shirt. Bentley was being more leisurely, taking off the dress shirt he was wearing carefully button by button, before folding it meticulously and setting it on one of the tables he'd brought in from the family room, his shirt covered over some of the things that sat there. Eddy was already naked before Bentley had even gotten his shoes off.

Patty got onto the table, stroking herself vigorously as she lay there, staring at Eddy languorously. Finally, she seemed tired of waiting, she held out a condom to Eddy, "Everybody plays safe in our playpen. Come here baby, why don't we get started while Mister Slowpoke finishes getting undressed? That's a hell of a cock there, and I feel so empty."

Eddy needed little encouragement. He took the condom and tore it open with his teeth. Before he could put it on himself, Patty reached up, "Let me, baby."

Eddy could not even believe his luck tonight as she took the condom from him and expertly rolled it over his cock. Normally this was work, but tonight, tonight he couldn't be more into it. Once it had reached the base, she kept a firm grip on his shaft and tugged him toward her. She placed him at her entrance, and he needed no encouragement at all. Eddy slammed his dick into Patty. He went in instantly, clearly, she was into it as well, she was soaked. He froze for a moment feeling her heat and moisture easily despite the latex between them.

"Holy shit Miss O'Neil, you are on fire!" he gasped before starting a rhythmic thrusting into her pussy.

"Slow down tiger," she gasped. "Player three is getting ready to enter, and then you'll really see me get into it."

As she spoke Eddy felt Bentley's hand on his shoulder. He glanced back to see the bigger man rolling a condom onto his manhood. Eddy could only feel grateful that this wasn't his first rodeo, even if few of them had been as wild as this. He quickly turned his head back to look at Miss O'Neil writhing underneath him. His fear evaporated, replaced by glorious anticipation.

"Don't worry, I'll take breaks if you need to," Bentley breathed in his ear. Just the hint of the forceful voice sent a shiver down Eddy's spine. He felt the man's rough fingers probing and lubing him in preparation and let out a groan. Eddy was shocked himself; he wasn't faking anything. If he had any money, tonight was the kind of thing he'd have paid for himself.

The fingers vanished, and he felt the latex-covered head of the man's cock at his asshole. Eddy forced himself to relax. Bentley pushed forward slowly and steadily, and just as easily Eddy's body knew from years of practice what to do, opening for the larger man like a flower. The slight pain of entrance ebbed once the head was inside.

Eddy couldn't take it anymore; the guy was going so slow it was like he was teasing him. Eddy slammed back onto the cock, so violently he almost removed himself from Patty's sweet snatch.

"Oh fuck!" Eddy gasped with pleasure. They stayed still and let the experience exist, transfixed from the moment of joining like a butterfly pinned to a mat. At last, Eddy got himself under control enough to gasp out, "Just stay still Bentley, and let me give you and Miss O'Neil a ride." Before the other man could say anything, Eddy had already settled into a bouncing motion, his cock thrusting down into Patty, then his ass slamming back onto Bentley's cock.

"Just....let me know....when you're going to come, so we can all come together," Bentley managed to grunt out, as he added little thrusts of his own to Eddy's own back thrusts.

It was almost a surprise Eddy heard him over the mewling moans Patty was letting out as he fucked her. "Sure thing boss, but it won't be long now."

Bentley leaned over the table, but Eddy mostly ignored him as a person, the man had been reduced to a cock, a totem of power that existed for Eddy's stimulation. He was in heaven; this was like some fucking dream come true. His dick slamming away into a female parental figure while a big old bear filled him inside. He only had eyes for Patty right now, watching as she twisted and contorted herself, impaled on his dick. This was about to be the best orgasm of his life right into the grasping cunt of authority.

He felt Bentley lean back away from the table, one of the man's hands grabbed his hip, he drove him further toward his peak. Eddy wondered for just a moment where Bentley's other hand was, but the sensations building up made the thought only a fleeting one. The act of dominating and being dominated in unison became a closed loop world view with which nothing could compete.

"I'm gonna cum! I can't hold it any longer," Eddy gasped.

They were his last words. Bentley drove the knife he had retrieved from under the table up under Eddy's chin piercing all the way to the man's brain with the force he drove it home with. When he yanked it out, Eddy's body spasmed, Bentley felt the blood run down his hands and heard it begin to splatter onto Patty. It was too much. He came, yanking the younger man's spurting head back as he thrust completely inside him, his own living body jerking with each spasm of orgasm brought on by the tremors of the dying body he was inside of.

It took him a long moment to register Patty's screams. It took even longer to register that they weren't screams of fear or revulsion. Patty was experiencing an orgasm powerful enough to bring the house down. Bentley looked past the already rotting flesh bag he held upright to take in the sight of her. She looked glorious, a smile of intense satisfaction on her face as she rubbed Eddy's blood into her breasts with one hand and used it as lubricant to stimulate her clit with the other.

He pulled out of Eddy and slowly removed the dead cock from Patty.

"I have never felt anything like that, ever. It's like I've been waiting for that for my entire life and when he came inside me and his life flowed all over me....." she whispered.

"And that's just for starters," Bentley smiled. "Normally I take their nose, their ears, sometimes their eyes and lips before they die. I make them what they are, interchangeable. I want them to know it before they die. But I knew you'd picked Eddy for a reason; I wanted you to relish it."

He was right. Eddy had used the boy she'd been trying to save. The kid had a bright and sunny disposition, despite all of the crap life had foisted on him for being gay. He had a future. That future wasn't with his intolerant father and the man's bowing and scraping girlfriend, that was for sure. But she kept trying to tell the kid, survive it two more years and go to college, and then fuck all of them. Once you're out the door, you're on to your future and they won't matter anymore. Instead, the poor thing had gone running to the streets looking for acceptance, a community. All he had found were users like Eddy and his dubious fellow travelers. She could tell just looking at Aiden once she'd found him and got him back that those scumbags had used the vulnerable kid for all he was worth. Even now his eyes had lost some of their sparkle, he would probably never get it back. They took that. She wanted Eddy dead, and now he was, the world had actually worked the way she thought it always should.

"Why'd you agree to do this out here," she asked.

"Because, when you told me you wanted to do one who was awake for all of it, once they're in the back room, they usually know the jig is up and they're in trouble. I wanted him to think he was getting one over on you again, and then I wanted to take it from him," Bentley said

"What now?"

"Now, we drag him to the meat hooks, hang him up and I field strip him. After that, you should probably get a shower and head home. We'll figure out who next later," he said.

"Home?"

"Well, my place is a pig stye," he grinned.

"It's not..."

"Don't insult my hard work. But also, it would look weird if Miss Perfect vanished from her apartment for days on end. People might get concerned. So, let's keep it looking normal for now, huh?" he said as he went to remove the false bit of wall that led to the real playroom.

He watched her car drive away on his cameras. It had been a hell of a night. Life had changed so much and in so short a period of time that it would need to be processed. Bentley already felt like he could tell her everything, what his vision was, why he did this. Common sense and the survival instincts that had allowed him to be above suspicion for years now told him not to. What she didn't need to know, he didn't need to tell her. She didn't need to know about the cameras yet, for instance. She didn't need to know about his second home, what he called a cabin, up in the hills above the city. All of that was a need-to-know basis, and if everything continued apace, she'd get there, it just wasn't for today.

Soon he felt that he could really make her understand how he saw them. There had been nothing special about Eddy, nothing truly human. He was a two-bit hustler and abuser; he filled a role. Society wanted them on all levels of the socio-economic strata to make the sheep timid with their money and belongings, thrifty. There were dozens of them in every city in every country on the planet. Each ran variations of the same games, each thinking they were slick and above it all. Exactly the same, though none of them had ever spoken, nothing unique or interesting. The only way to make someone like Eddy interesting was to make him scream in agony as you removed the disguise of humanity he wore. The "features" they had no need of and didn't deserve. Only when you created the blank canvas, that empty vessel ready to accept your seed, only then were they worth giving a flying fuck about. You could taste their pain at that moment, the only original and interesting expressions of self they'd ever been capable of in their lives. And when they finally died, like the livestock they were, they'd fill your larder.

Still, tonight had been fun. It had been the most fun

when he had been listening to her cries as she came and came again, Bentley knew what little drone Patty had inside her was dying, falling away like a cracked chrysalis. He could expect her call soon, wanting to go again. He'd have to train her in secrecy, but that was all right, she already had good ideas in that direction. He'd learned by doing, he could use that to speed things up for her. Watching the pleasure she took from bathing in Eddy's excuse of a life made all the extra work worthwhile.

Even thinking about his day after she left was legitimately stimulating. This was not too unusual, he often found himself reminiscing and needing some private time. Not the urge to kill, he had a layer of emotional removal from that. He noticed the hard-on he had already, Patty was something he was into in a way he had only been once before in life. And Patty had no reason to leave him, Patty was an active participant now, not a victim. Groping at his stiffening wood, he decided this called for a special treat down in the room.

He removed his clothing in the tool room and went into the inner chamber naked. Continuing past the table he went through to the bone room. All the drones, showing how boring they really were stacked up here, not even a stunted limb among them to make them interesting. A drone could go through his whole life shaking hands and saying, "Hi, I'm so and so, I blah blah!" and think it mattered worth a shit in the grand scheme of things. But here, here with the bones categorized by bone and not by person, you'd need special equipment to put a name to anyone.

Bentley carefully removed a radius from the pile of arm bones. He knew exactly which one he wanted. He returned to the chamber and positioned the table he had brought back exactly how he wanted it and climbed up. This piece of arm was a bit more polished at one end, to ensure there was no chipping or fraying of bone. He let a bit of lube drip onto the shining surface and rubbed it all over the mushroom-like top of the bone.

"Ahh!" he gasped a little as the flared head of the bone made its way past his anus. The radius was almost built for this he'd discovered one day when he let his curiosity run free. The flared head making entrance sent a shiver, but even more so, a slight flare out in the bone a little beyond that, it seemed designed as a prosthetic as it rubbed against the prostate perfectly.

His cock, despite the previous fucking it had done, almost ached with desire already. With one hand he began to stroke it. With the other, he used the distal end of the bone to begin to fuck himself. It was like the bone was designed as a sex toy as much as an actual arm bone, even a handle on one end to really be able to pound with it.

Despite multiple orgasms on the day, it didn't take long with his toy's help. Soon cum spurted once and then oozed out of his overused balls. He let the bone work itself out of his anus. Eventually, he felt it plop onto the table. At least this clean-up wouldn't take as long as the previous one.

As he set the bone back in its place of honor, he lamented again that he couldn't remember the bone's donor. It was probably the one useful thing they'd ever provided the world and he couldn't for the life of him recall their name. Before he left, he prized three teeth out of one of the skulls. He'd powder them and toss them in a smoothie for himself. He needed to keep his strength up and extra calcium always helped. One less vitamin on the shopping list.

Patty lay in her bed pondering everything that had happened. So much, too much it felt to completely wrap your head around it all. Her day had started with the feeling that she was playing some game. She was the great Nancy Drew on the case. Yes, she had known what she had told herself about wanting to join him, but how could she believe that would really happen? No, she had been sleuthing, being clever, expecting to leave that house with evidence but still retaining all the opportunities to wuss out.

Until she lay there about to become his next victim.

Lying here now she contemplated Bentley; she could see what he meant about the faceless masses. She was supposed to scream, to cry, to plead. That was her role that life had picked out for her, simpering maiden.

She hadn't, she begged for something else, something only he could give her. And instead of slicing her apart, he had given her the greatest gift of all.

All her life there had been disappointment and being talked down to. Her father, the men she had dated in college, her co-workers, judges, all of them viewed anything she thought as "cute." Not because it was cute, but because she was just a girl to them, a pet. And then, when she had muscled her way past all of that it had turned out that for every person she saved, there was someone else looking to drag them even lower than they'd ever been. And it was all so predictable and repetitious. Every one of them thought they brought something special to the party, all of them brought the same crap as the last one. Those from her past, those from her present, and change the circumstance of their upbringing and you could even exchange them. Dullards who took what they wanted not because of merit, but because society had been built to let them do it,

None of that mattered when she felt the blood flow over her, her senses bubbled like her own blood was full of champagne. Sexual nerve endings that had never been touched before had been rubbed raw. Institutional power wasn't power, it was a gift of circumstance, feeling a virile man's blood pour over you while his cum shot into you, that was all the life force in the universe in one instant.

She had never felt as full and as satisfied with the world and her place in it as she did right now.

Bentley had done that for her.

Chapter 5

Not knowing what else to do, Patty decided that playing hard to get was a waste and called him two days later.

"Hey," she breathed when he answered. She was surprised by her own behavior, she found she wanted to sound attractive to him over the phone. How much could change and how quickly.

She could hear him smile through the phone when he replied, "Hey yourself, I was almost wondering if I'd hear from you again."

"Are you kidding? The only reason I didn't call before was that I didn't want to seem like some crazy stalker chick," she laughed lightly.

Bentley laughed back, "You know, I have never considered the possibility of that becoming a problem in my life before now."

"No, no I suppose you haven't"

"Hey," he said suddenly, "I was wondering if you could do me a favor?"

"Oh?" her heart rate thrilled just a little, the last time he had wanted something from her, he had given her even more back. It might be mundane this time, but even the possibility thrilled her.

"Look, could you come over tonight? I'm at work right now, I can ask you then," he said.

"Sure, I'll be by at seven." She hung up and tried to

consider how she'd contain herself until then.

He let her in the door shortly after seven.

"So, what's the big ask?" she demanded immediately.

Bentley looked a little shy for a moment, "Well, look, I've been thinking. I want you to feel comfortable in other parts of the house. Like, if this is going to work, we can't just fuck and kill, as fun as that is. A relationship also involves just hanging out, you know, talking, watching movies, things like that. I was thinking I'd ask for your expertise. How far do I really need to go? I mean to keep that hoarder look without all of the other shit that goes with it? I mean, how much would you, as a professional, need to see before you made that judgment call?"

Patty was taken aback by that; it certainly wasn't what she'd been expecting. Once she got over her initial surprise she felt touched by the gesture. They'd only spent a few hours together, and he was already willing to make a major life concession toward her comfort. Even without the more important thing they had shared, Bentley had put himself ahead of her last five boyfriends.

"I honestly mean it when I say that really touches me, Bentley," she smiled. "Sure, I can help you with that, we can give it the glow of a shut-in, without so much of the blow."

Bentley smiled back at her; happy he'd pleased her. "So, where do we start?"

"Kitchen, absolutely the kitchen. First off, some of the smell is going to linger anyway, secondly, you went overboard there," she replied instantly.

Bentley raised an eyebrow, "How so?"

"The water for starters, you don't need to leave water in the sink. Heck, if you just stacked some dishes you didn't care about and moved them from time to time, you'd still have your sink. Probably want to burn some of that trash, you don't need that much," she explained. "You're aiming for hoarder, not crack house."

"OK, when do we get started? You point, I heave-ho."

Patty's anticipation was at a fever pitch when she heard the car door slam upstairs in the garage. She had been a part of a kill that was done for her benefit, and it had filled a hole she had only suspected she had in her life, it left her anticipating. Anticipating life again. Tonight, would be different, tonight she was going to get to watch him work, to help him in his work. She was going to see what Bentley needed for himself in a kill firsthand.

She heard two sets of footsteps coming down the basement steps which surprised her. What she'd seen of his work before involved an unconscious victim. She sat on the table, her feet drummed on the floor in anticipation as she waited.

The door opened; Bentley stepped in with a young man in his early 20s slumped over his shoulder. The boy was conscious, but only barely. His hair hung dankly into his face, but what she could see of it revealed a set of eyes that were half-mast at best.

Bentley saw her staring. "I bought him a couple of drinks. Good stamina though, he made it to the family room. Help me with him," he grinned.

She hopped off the table and Bentley lay the young man down. Working together they quickly stripped his filthy clothes away, tossing them in a corner before strapping down each exposed limb as it came free. Once the young man was locked in place, Patty could get a better look at him. In her estimation he wasn't a junkie, his arms looked too clean for that, and while there were scars, they weren't drug scars. They weren't tracks or bowl burns, they looked like cuts and slashes. He was an adult, but only barely. If she had to guess, she'd guess a former runaway who never went home. Instead of returning to whatever agonies lay back where he'd come from, he'd learned how to survive in a new environment and found an evolutionary niche. He had that half-starved look to him that models try so hard to achieve, a look that street people get for free. With a bath, some mood lighting, and the right clothes he could be a sex symbol.

As they finished strapping the now naked boy

down, Patty asked, "So what are we doing tonight?"

"I got him for you, I want you to enjoy him once I make it look like they all look to me," Bentley replied.

Patty looked at the boy's flaccid penis, "I don't know how much I can do with that. Especially after you start cutting him up."

Bentley reached over to a rolling table nearby where he had laid out what he expected to use. He came back holding a syringe, "I mixed up a little helper for him. A mix of Trazodone and Mirtazapine, both have been known to cause a full painful rager on their own, together they've been known to blow right by a normal tolerance. Let's see what they do to our playmate, shall we?"

Patty smiled at him as he injected the boy in the arm with it.

"I'd put it in his cock directly, but it's tricky to hit the right artery. Why those guys who shot themselves up with coke back in the day thought it would work is beyond me. You might want to give him a few strokes to help him rise," Bentley said almost clinically before turning back to his other tools.

When he turned back again the boy's penis was hard and had turned a painful-looking reddish purple. "Well, it looks like he's good for you to use as you like my dear. Now, if you'll let me work, I'll let you finally see them as I see them."

Patty didn't need any encouragement. Even the

thought of doing something like this had energized her sexually, it charged her like nothing had since the night she had lost her virginity in what was half a fumbling attempt at sex and half rape. It always felt like that, like it was a duty to be performed, an acquiescence to a stronger force in the world. Somehow knowing Bentley could kill her had made the sex with him incredible, and since then, knowing her partner was dying had made it unreal. Seeing the young man strapped down and helpless and seeing his cock throbbing in the open air had been more than she needed. Her clothes were quickly off and folded behind her.

She let out a satisfied moan as she climbed up on the table and sank herself onto the practically burning member.

Bentley let her grind for a little while as he enjoyed the view. He had to admit she looked sexy as all hell as she used the flesh tube, he could feel himself coming to attention. The needs of the little head would have to wait, he had work to do for the big one. He wanted her to see, to understand, and hopefully accept.

It was hard to shut out the little moans and gasps she let out as he selected his tools. For now, a scalpel would do. He didn't need to hurt this one too much yet. In fact, the kid was still out cold, how much of a reaction he'd even get out of him was questionable. He'd see once the heavy stuff started, but first, it was time for a haircut.

He fired up a set of hair clippers, Patty opened her

eyes for a second at the sound, but then smiled and went back to working the cock inside her. Bentley had done this before enough times to be the model of efficiency; he removed the hair from the young man's head with long drags of the clipper letting it fall to the floor in greasy clumps. After their playmate was bald, he also removed the eyebrows. He was thankful he'd dosed the kid up well; Bentley wasn't sure if Patty was ready for the screaming that would normally be starting soon.

Next up, Bentley worked the scalpel between the helix and temporal muscle of the ear and began to cut. In many ways a larger blade worked easier for the removal of the ear, there was a lot of flesh and cartilage to work through. These days though, he tried to make things cleaner when he could, he found that ragged edges became distinguishing marks that defeated the purpose. Also, those kinds of gashing cuts were harder to close if he wanted them to last a little while.

Blood pooled and dripped from the slashed flesh as he threw the detached ear into a nearby bucket. Next, he picked up a small blowtorch. His hands were slippery with blood, so it took a few tries to get the thing lit, the clicking of the sparker was erratic as his hands slipped. Once it was finally going, he twisted the nob a bit to get the hottest, tightest flame possible. When he applied the flame to the side of the boy's head he was surprised when the body gave a small twitch and a whimper. Well, something to note, scorching the wound closed hurt more than the actual wound. Wasn't that just the way life worked? Full of cures that hurt more than the disease ever had? The smell of burnt flesh hit his nose giving him a cosey feeling, like the scent of chestnuts at Christmas.

The other ear went the same. He looked up to see Patty smiling at him as he worked while she continued to grind against the victim's member. His hand came up with something he'd bought last year, one of a set of stainless-steel evisceration spoons. They worked perfectly for what came next. Pulling back the eyelid he inserted the spoon down and under the eye. With one hand he pried the eyelid open as wide as it would go, with the other he deftly popped the eyeball out of its socket. As drugged as this one was, he wondered if this created any stimuli that entered into the dreamworld the brain currently resided in.

He looked up to see Patty watching him work and pinching her nipples.

A moment later the other eyeball came out. Thankfully he didn't need the torch for this. It bled, but nothing that would bring the party to a premature end. On the other hand, he would need the torch for the next part. The scalpel in hand again, he began to work on the nose. Again, he worked carefully, like a surgeon really. Bentley moved the scalpel smoothly along the nostrils and up to the ridge feeling it catch here or there on a piece of cartilage. He felt carefully around until he was sure he'd located where the nasal tip joined to the skull. For this next bit, he traded out his scalpel for a set of what looked like wire cutters. A loud crack, loud enough to make Patty jump a bit, and the nose came off free in his hand. A quick application of the torch and the bleeding stopped.

The drone on the table let out a moan.

"I think he might be coming around," Bentley noted.

Patty smiled at him, "Hand me the scalpel and then I want you to do something fun,"

"Oh?"

"Fuck me up the ass, I want to feel both of you. Just take your time, all right? I haven't let anyone do that in a very long time," she replied as she continued to grind on the body below her.

Now that Bentley was done with him, she could finally see what he meant about them. At least she thought she did. With the distinguishing features removed, what exactly was the difference between this guy and the dozens she'd already seen pass through the system in her five years as a caseworker? And not just her, but each of the case workers on her team. Multiply it by every city in the country.... All those identical stories heading toward predictable endings. At least, until Bentley came along and imparted full-blown distinguishment on them, the only way they could achieve it. By being a sacrifice.

She felt Bentley take her hand and place the scalpel in it, "Be careful with it, huh?"

She smiled, "You do the same back there, huh?"

Bentley was impressed, it appeared that she wanted to do her first kill tonight. He was also impressed by what she wanted him to do. In college that had taken pleading to get, unless the girl he was with was Catholic, then ANYTHING took pleading to get, but that was more likely. Doing it to Patty changed the paradigm for him as well. Normally when he did this, what did he care about the feelings of a faceless drone? By then he'd usually done so much to them that anal pain was the least of their worries. Now he'd need to be careful, take his time, make sure she enjoyed every second of tonight. Bentley almost felt performance anxiety as he began to lube his cock.

First, he stuck a lubed finger carefully into her anus, he felt it contract and send off waves of heat as he made sure she was well-greased to receive him. Withdrawing the digit, he replaced it with the head of his prick, now throbbing and ready. With as much self-control as he could manage, he said, "You sure about this?"

"Do it, just be careful putting it in," she gasped, her face rosy with lust and her breathing increasing with anticipation.

He pushed forward slowly but steadily; she grunted a little as he began to stretch her. Finally, the head of his cock passed the barrier of her ring into the heated depths beyond, and he sunk into her.

"Hold it for just a second baby, let me adjust a bit. I have never felt this full in my life," she gasped.

He clutched tightly at her hips; it was all he could do to not pound her now.

"I'm ready, fuck me, baby, fuck me good," she sighed. "Let me know when you're going to cum, and make it loud, because I plan to do some screaming."

She didn't lie, she caterwauled as he plowed her ass. He could feel the other man's cock in her pussy rubbing against his with each thrust. The upward pressure flicking the underside of his own penis was wiping out his staying power.

A voice muttered, "Where am I?"

He looked past Patty to see the faceless one tossing his head from side to side in confusion. Patty got even louder when she noticed.

She calmed herself just enough to lean into the drone and say, "Don't worry baby, mamma's got you."

"I'm going to cum soon" Bentley grunted.

"Perfect," Patty replied.

As he continued to fuck her, he watched as she pushed herself up. Taking the scalpel in one hand, with surprising precision considering how hard he was banging into her, she carefully exposed the trachea with a downward slice.

"Oh my God! What are you doing? Why can't I see?" moaned the faceless one.

In two lighting fast motions first Patty sliced directly across the trachea causing the young man's panicked breathing to come whistling out through the hole. Arching back, she immediately stabbed the scalpel down, fitting it smoothly between the 4th and 5th rib. Withdrawing the blade and setting it aside, she slammed her mouth down onto the wound in the throat. It was all too much for Bentley, he came as hard as he could ever remember cumming before clutching onto her hips like she was a life preserver.

They all lay there for a long moment, Patty twitched as she had a series of subsiding orgasms. Bentley didn't move at all except for great gasps for air. Finally, he found the strength to pull himself off her back and pull out. A little bit after that Patty used her newborn fawn weak and shaky legs to get off the still-swollen member of the corpse she was on.

"What did you do?" he asked her as she leaned back against him for support.

"I wanted to taste its dying breath," she smiled, blood covering her lips, and smeared onto her face.

Bentley glowed inside at that.

Bentley recovered first and went back to the cooling body on the table. He grabbed a scalpel first, which he used to make a series of cuts around the anus. In the process, he removed the faceless one's still erect penis and testes and set them aside. He looked carefully to ensure that both the bladder and the intestines had been cut free and were just sitting on the pelvis loosely. Next, he turned his attention to making a cut along the sternum, blood oozed up, but with no heart pumping it, all it did was ooze. Satisfied, he thrust his fingers under the skin over the abdominal wall.

"What are you doing?" Patty said once she came down from her own cloud.

"Field stripping out the guts. Say, you aren't partial to any organs, are you? I mean as food?"

She shook her head, "No, I hate liver, kidneys, and heart, all of it tastes gross."

"I wouldn't be too confident on the flavor of this particular specimen especially," he agreed. That decided he retrieved another blade and reached into the gap he'd created between the muscle wall and the skin with it. A series of swift slashes worked his way the rest of the way down to the hole he had created earlier when he'd cut off the penis.

"Now let's see, next the sternum," Bentley said conversationally. He picked up a handheld small saw. "Battery operated, which makes life so much easier. It's about to get loud."

He hadn't lied, the saw whirred to life with the sound of an electric drill before changing to the horrid grind as it worked its way along the sternum, creating little grinding crunches as bits of bone snapped off or ground away. Every move he had made up until now had reduced their victim even further in Patty's eyes, but somehow that grinding noise brought back what Bentley was actually doing. She was just about to cover her ears and turn away when the noise cut out.

Bentley used both hands and spread back the rib cage and reached inside with the scalpel again. "On to the next bit, all we need to do is cut loose the heart sack, like so. Then we cut the esophagus like that, and hey, you got part of that already, so even easier. Finally, we hack out the diaphragm and we're left with nothing but a bowl of guts!"

"Now what?" she asked with genuine curiosity.

"Now my dear, all I need to do is wrap his wrists with wire. Get the catch pan under him. And finally use the hook to winch him up. Everything should fall right out," he said pleasantly, already winding wire around the young man's wrists.

As the clacking noise of the winch began, Patty quickly moved back. It was funny, she didn't mind, no she reveled in their blood when she killed them, but not now. Now that it had cooled the blood and viscera seemed vile, like refuse. Achieving a death was beautiful, sublime. Eating the flesh was waste not, want not, stacking the bones was even fine, being splashed by congealing blood or an organ made her shudder. She was well back before the first moist thump hit the pan.

Once Bentley had the body hung up, he began cutting smooth lines around the wrist and down the arms with a scalpel. Patty watched as he picked up a different knife and began working the skin off the red threads of the arm meat with little flicks of the blade as he went. She had to wonder at how easily the skin came away. Just a few cuts and a continuing series of flicks of the blade and this was becoming even less than faceless. It was just meat waiting for the butcher to do his vital and holy work.

He did the other arm as well, whistling as he went. Once the skin had been flensed away exposing the veins and muscles that made the meat of the right arm he said, "Going to do the head next. The temptation is to just do like the hands and feet and let the peroxide do its work, but really, I've found it goes smoother if I skin it. Not to mention, there are some pretty good straps of meat on the neck and around the jaw. Marinade it for a while and it makes excellent jerky."

The skinning didn't bother her nearly as much as the gutting had, but she still had to ask, "Bentley, why are you showing me all of this?"

"You're my partner babe. I want you to be able to handle all aspects of this. But not only that, we're hunters, Patty. Really, at the end of the day, that's what we do. We're thinning the herd of drones, the ones that don't deserve a face. The thing there is, every good hunter should respect their prey. That's why we eat the meat, so we can treat them like a sacred bounty that lasts for more than the time it takes us to fuck them. I find that when I'm stripping them down like this, I find myself thankful that enough of them exist that they won't miss a few. That this body has given me pleasure, and now it will make me strong. It helps you find the sacredness of our duty, the fortitude to remove these faceless creatures from a world they would overpopulate without us. You have the time to think about the fact that this drone has already been replaced, and without your work, they'd overrun the actual people of the world," he replied earnestly.

"I don't know about gutting them...."

"I know, it isn't really pleasant, but we're conditioned to think guts are gross," he said, setting down his tools and going to the pan. He held up the purple bulge of a kidney, "But really, what's so gross about it? It's just a wet thing, and we touch them all time. The tactile sensation isn't so different from a wet rag or sponge. We're conditioned to think they're gross. And the drones were the ones who conditioned us, so anything from them we can rid ourselves of as well."

They were both quiet for a minute as Bentley dropped the kidney and wiped off his hands. He smiled when he looked at her in contemplation of what he'd just said. "Want to help me with the rest of the skinning? Get a real feel for it?"

"OK," she replied quietly and timidly. While she had risen to every challenge so far, a week ago she'd been a mere mild-mannered social worker. Every step she took was one she pushed herself to make. The rewards had been commensurate, but she wondered what her limit would be.

"Great!" he enthused. "I'm going to put some slices here on shoulders. We don't need the pelt for anything, so it will make it a little easier. Since we have the ribcage spread, why don't you work back from there?"

He handed her the knife and held the skin above the ribcage back a little bit for her. She slid the knife in with a shaky hand and moved it sideways. She stopped when she felt how easily it moved, how tenuous our body's grasp was on our own skin. She moved it a little more, and it slid below the dermis, the hypodermis turning out to be a flimsy and weak connector to the muscle below. In fact, she found a giggle of glee rising up as a large flap of skin peeled back exposing the muscle-covered ribs that had never been meant to see the light of day. This had nothing to do with murder, this was turning flesh into meat, and she was discovering a skill here. One she never would have known if not for Bentley's gentle coaxing.

"You're a natural at this Patty!" Bentley enthused. "We're almost ready to do the other side, and it seems like I only just handed you the knife."

"I am a woman of hidden talents," she smiled coquettishly.

"Well, for showing me your hidden talents, I suppose you deserve a treat," he said.

"Like what?"

"How bout I show you what's behind the other door?" he grinned.

"Ooooooo do I get a secret decoder ring too?"

Chapter 6

Hare was having a shitty day. A legitimate one, part of being a cop was knowing the difference between a shitty day and just run of the mill SNAFU. First off, his doer on one of his official cases ended up having an airtight alibi as to their location the night of the assault. Secondly, his favorite deli ran out of Swiss cheese right before he pulled up to order his normal ham and Swiss on rye. Finally, he got back to the station and was going over the latest figures on his little project and it looked like his project had every reason to be continued. While any set of lists pertaining to any crimes in the city's lower social strata could be considered nebulous at best, these seemed to show a definite trend. Even more of the bottom rung of hookers and dealers were playing hide and seek with the world than normal. The big question was, where the hell did they go?

Life wasn't like some shit box cop show where you followed well-placed clues, rookies had to be dissuaded of that illusion early on. Cops didn't know all of the perpetual lowlifes and no-hopers on their beat when they needed a handy suspect or informant. For fuck's sake, in the parts of the city that seemed to be getting depleted, you didn't even get out of your car if you could help it. In those parts of any city, there was only a 50-50 chance that the denizens would react with fear when seeing a badge. And if they didn't? Most of the fuckers were better armed than you were. So, you rolled on by in your cruiser and kept your head down if you wanted to see retirement.

Unless there was a murder, and it was actually reported that was. Then, you roped off the area and you called the Detectives in, Hare for instance. For as much as they even were detectives when it came to slum crime. Hare had been called into those parts of the city enough times to feel like he was pissing in the wind. You weren't doing detective work down there. Sherlock Holmes would have finally just OD'ed and been done with it if he'd had to work those cases. You showed up, you asked the gawkers if anyone had seen anything, you checked for a significant other to pin it on, and barring some miracle of God you were calling the case shelved before the body made it to the morgue.

But still, when there was a roust to keep the arrest numbers up, you got used to seeing the same old names float across. These people were in a bucket and couldn't crawl out, they didn't have the resources, and sooner or later they stopped having hope. When that happened, a downward spiral began. If you picked one up this week on "Let's pad our numbers night," you could count on them being on the next report too. If you didn't see their names on the arrest report, you saw it on a toe tag down in the morgue. That was how the sausage was made.

Hare couldn't say why he cared, his job had always been to try and put the very people he was worrying about in jail. At first, he had just noticed the missing familiar faces and got curious. But now that he had started nosing around, he was sure he was on to something. But what in the hell was he on to? If it was a serial killer, common sense said he'd have at least seen a body or two come in. Nobody hides their kills that well, hell, the vast majority of the monsters wanted you to see what they did. So why were the faces missing from the street and the bodies missing from the damned morgue?

He shut down his computer swearing he was done with it this time. Just like he'd sworn he was done the last five times he'd crunched the numbers. It was the way he'd just lie to himself like that that drove him to drink.

The door was thick and lined with metal. It clanged and clanked as he unlocked it and pulled it open.

"I'm like a little girl on Christmas," Patty enthused.

"It's nothing that great yet, but it could be," he replied as he turned on the lights.

What she was presented with was a set of steps. At the bottom, she could see a brightly lit room but not much else. Judging from the number of steps leading down, quite a large room. For some reason, even though she was already well and truly under the earth in a cave Bentley had hollowed out himself, the concept of going deeper into the earth gave her a momentary shudder of claustrophobia. Patty caught herself and closed off that part of her brain snapping at it to shut up like a parent with a misbehaving child. Every step of the way toward her new freedom was a test, and she would not be tripped up by something as stupid as this.

Bentley paused, already halfway down the wood and concrete stairs, "You coming?"

She smiled a little too brightly, "Sorry, wanted to give my eyes a second to adjust so I don't go tumbling down into you."

He smiled back, "Well, then I appreciate your consideration for my well-being."

She got herself back under control and followed him down the steps. When the large room finally came completely into view, she froze trying to understand what she was looking at. Fear for her own safety made her heart rate speed up. She managed to hold the fear back and her voice sounded amazed more than frightened when she asked, "So, what in the world?"

What it was, was a large square white room containing two large cells. Each cell held a spartan toilet, a shower, and a cot. Both were enclosed by large steel bars, and there were metal rings embedded in different spots in the walls and hooked to the bars of the cages. It was all unused, and of recent construction, it had a new house smell that assaulted the nostrils in this closed-off sub-basement. That mix of glues and paint that lingers in the air until a place is properly lived in that informed the nostrils that this place had never known humanity except in the building of it.

"I had the idea a while ago. My dad owned a construction company, among other things. I had all this put in when I inherited the house. I overbuilt because I wasn't sure what I'd be doing. Over time I've added some things down here in this room to maybe keep a couple of drones. Sooner or later the police are going to pick up on the missing scumbags just like you said. You'll help, everyone won't have to be a street hustler anymore. But still, while killing them is the ultimate rush, you have to admit, the using them before then feels mighty fine as well. So, I figured, why not keep a couple, take our time removing the features they don't deserve, keep them down here, and keep them fed for our lean times," he said his arm sweeping in a grand gesture.

"But, I mean, how tractable will they even be if we're holding them captive?" she wondered.

"Very, at least eventually. We'll be their only source of sensation, suddenly blind, no sound down except what we provide, only a few feet of space to explore. I plan to put in a TV to keep them from going totally mad, but that won't make it all better. A few days of that existence and even brutal sex will feel like something. Add in some positive reinforcement, something as stupid as ice cream or something, and they'll be begging for it every time we come down here to feed them. There are no indomitable wills, everything and everyone has limits. Most people usually are ashamed to find out how low their limit is," he said assuredly.

"A TV isn't a bad idea; you can use the programming as a rewards program. But, speaking of noise...."

"You kidding? This thing is so well soundproofed you could be in the kitchen upstairs and I could set off a bomb down here and you'd never know it." She could see the pride on his face, it told her that he'd thought of everything.

She had to admit he was right too. Yes, cities provided so many bottom-rung scum feeders, but if they took too many without taking breaks, even the dimmest flat foot might notice something weird. It wouldn't be the same, it couldn't be the same as the kill. But staring at those changed faces as they pleasured you would take the edge off the need for a while. Maybe you couldn't take everything from them all at once, but you could take a little bit every time as a taste.

"So, when do we get a boy toy to put in the first cell?"

"I knew you'd understand."

They were still debating on who to cull from the herd as their new pet. Well, it wasn't that, as much as Patty wanted it to be perfect. If everything worked out, they'd be living with this drone for some time. Bentley would have grabbed the first available drone that he could stand, she was seeing it long-term. It wasn't a matter of appearance, whatever they looked like now was going to be removed forever. It also wasn't a matter of personality, if they were on Patty's radar, they were already weak-willed and looking for the easy way through life. One thing that was a larger concern was a matter of health, could they survive the preparation for the cage? They couldn't just grab any old junkie for this, their system would collapse from the shock. Imagine detoxing and fighting infection and shock from a sliced-off nose at the same time, you need to be hardy for something like that.

And now, today was a new adventure for her. Bentley had provided her with a set of directions and asked that she meet him there. Now that she had them plugged into her maps feature, she couldn't help but wonder if this was her being sent on some scavenger hunt as a joke. The city continued to drop away, and yet according to Google she still had miles to go. She couldn't help but suspect this was a test to see how willing she was to let go of control and follow orders. Bentley's house was on the outer edge of the burbs where people still owned fields, but this.... This was nowhere.

Her car had been climbing steadily for a while now, deeper and higher into woods she'd never visited before in her life. In a way she was amazed, this mountainous forest primeval had been right there and she'd been as clueless as every other city dweller as to its existence. She was afraid to look at her phone, fearful she'd have no bars at all. Patty didn't want to be reminded of how much she had come to rely on technology to keep her feeling connected to the world, how it kept you somehow safer. For all her disdain for how the world was, this trip was teaching her one thing, she relied on that world more than she had ever admitted to herself before.

She was almost ready to give up and go home, especially when she realized Google didn't know where she was anymore, and she'd resorted to using a paper map she'd bought at Bentley's suggestion. She pulled off into a driveway to consider her next move, whether to find a signal and call Bentley or just go home in a huff. She took a moment to take in her surroundings a bit. That was when she saw the number on the post at the end of the drive. Grabbing her phone, she double-checked the address he'd texted her.

Kismet, she was meant to find the place. She put her car in gear and slowly began her way up the dirt drive as it dove under the limbs of trees that had been ancient when her grandparents had wed. The woods gave the world a green glow as she drove through the dusk they created. Where there had been rainbows of color in the world down on the main road, she found herself driving in a place that only had grays and browns and green. As she rounded a bend, she could see bright sunlight ahead. She didn't even notice as she gave the car some gas in her rush to finally return to the sun.

Sitting on the steps of the cabin that greeted her was Bentley, smoking a cigar. The forest had been cut back from all sides of the cabin, creating an oasis of bright light. Her eyes were partially blinded by the sudden burst of sunlight causing her to squint at first until they adjusted. The log cabin itself looked like a prefab, a little too precise a little too clean cut, but still, it was a wondrously large rustic building, with a second-floor balcony over the large front porch. Behind it, tucked more into the woods, was a barn of similar construction. Bentley stood up as she pulled the car into a spot next to his SUV.

When she got out he beamed at her and said, "I had one more surprise for you. My home away from home."

"It looks lovely," she replied coming up to hug him.

He kissed her quickly before saying, "Well, don't get too comfy yet, this is a working trip. I'll give you the grand tour in a minute, but first I'll show you what we're up to here today."

She followed him behind the house toward the barn that up close looked more like it was used for storage than animals. In front of it was a contraption bolted to some kind of flat wooden wagon. She tried to puzzle it out but she couldn't decide what its use could possibly be. Bentley reached behind it and brought out a large rattling duffle bag, when he unzipped it there was no mistaking what was inside, bones.

"You get a backlog of the things. So, I built a crusher setup. It'll get everything down to powder. The powder is great for your garden, but not just that, I have a few places I can dispose of it where it will never be noticed. I know none of this is as easy as just dumping a body in a river, but hey, where's the fun in that I say? They keep me company for a while.... but all good things must end. Think of it as using the whole animal, we fuck them, we kill them, we eat them, and then they help grow food for us. If they had their own way about their disposal, they'd let themselves be turned into poison and ruin a perfectly good plot of land," Bentley explained.

"That's actually pretty cool. I take it this goes easier with two, otherwise, why have me up here? So, what's my role?" Patty asked.

"In all honesty, I wanted to show you the cabin. I thought we'd spend the night. But while we're here.... the sloppy killers get the chair; the tidy ones get to laugh forever. Basically, there are two jobs if we want it to go fast. You can either feed the machine or smack the bones with a hammer to break them down, you're the guest today, your call," he smiled back.

"I don't know how good I'd be with the hammer...."

"You sure you'll be fine with the machine?"

"I guess, it's either or, right?"

He nodded, "True. Let me fire it up, and I'll do the

first few, and then you can step in. How's that sound?"

"Sounds like a plan," Patty smiled

Bentley turned on the little one-stroke motor and it began to make a rattling and clacking immediately. As soon as the motor was up and running smoothly, he pulled one of the bones out of the gunny sack. It looked to be a leg bone. Carefully he placed it on an anvil he'd bolted to a bench he brought out next to the machine. The hammer he picked up looked to be heavy and all business, one side ending with a flat surface, the other ending in a spike. Bentley reared back and swung. A crack could be heard even above the din of the motor. He slammed the hammer down on the bone again before setting it down. He took the three pieces of bone and tossed them into a chute on the machine. A hideous grinding noise rose up for just a moment before Patty could see a cloud of white dust pluming up from the bag that was hooked up underneath it.

Bentley repeated the process and yelled to her, "Pretty simple, huh?"

"Seems to be!" she yelled back, moving to get next to him at the bench.

"Here, put on some safety goggles, and we'll be done in no time," he said as he held up a pair of plastic goggles for her.

Bentley had had four of those bags in his vehicle. It had taken the best part of the afternoon to finally reduce the bones to so much fertilizer, but they were finally done. Both of them were coated in a fine white dust from their efforts only interrupted by streaks of sweat.

"Why don't I show you to the shower, and I can get our clothes into the washer," Bentley said, leading her up the steps into the cabin.

"Better idea, why don't you join me in the shower, and then we can luxuriate naked and clean while the clothes wash."

"I like your idea better," he smiled. He leaned down to kiss her, the grit from the bones creating a weird sensation as the skin around their lips touched. Even so, she felt a warmth spreading out from her stomach and down.

"Better yet, let's get a little dirtier before we get clean."

Their physical urges quenched, and their bodies cleaned, Patty let her eyes wander around the cabin to try and take it in. It really drove home the point of how much the mess at his main house was just a sham. The cabin wasn't immaculate, it wasn't lived in full time, keeping all the dust down would be impossible, but it was neat as a pin. Everything was in its place and had a place. Despite it being only a part-time house, there was barely that much of the expected dust on the shelves. She could only assume Bentley would dust at some point while they were up here.

He had gotten a fire going in the fireplace when she decided to ask, "How can you stand it?"

"Stand what?"

"The other house, the mess. I mean I know why it's a mess, but considering how tidy this place is...." her voice trailed off with a wave of her hand.

He nodded, "That's one of the things that separates us from the faceless ones, strength of will. I know why I want the house that way, it serves a purpose. I don't have to like it; I have to buckle down and deal with it if I want the advantages it provides. And hey! Thanks to you the overkill has been removed. The place is a lot more tolerable now."

"So why even use your home, why not take them up here?"

Bentley nodded again, "In theory that would be better, but there are two problems with up here. There's some nasty bedrock, it's difficult to even put in more than a rudimentary basement. It would make putting in the setup like the house unfeasible, at least damned difficult. Secondly, think of how long a drive that was. Imagine keeping somebody under that long. And out here, everybody knows everybody, people don't just vanish and have nobody care about it."

What he didn't add was that the house outside the suburbs was his parents' house. The parents who molded him, showed him the light, made him what he would become. Some part of him felt like there was no place better for his mission. No place had that feeling of a shrine as much as the house that had her room in it. He wasn't going to say that though, some things you know instinctively to keep to yourself no matter how secure you feel with another person. Some thoughts are only safe in the black hole at the center of your heart.

Finally, Patty decided she had the perfect target to be their keeper drone. One of her kid's mothers had gotten into hock with a local dealer. The guy wasn't a street dealer, he dealt out of his apartment, which meant larger amounts of both money and drugs. The guy had more on hand, and he had better quality, which cost more. The woman, a five-time loser in treatment, had started buying from him instead of off the street, probably to prove to herself she wasn't a junkie. She was just buying some off a friend, and could a junkie afford to do that? She couldn't prove it, but Patty was pretty sure the woman had been doing some light partying at the guy's place and he offered her that taste of something harder that would put her right back on the roller coaster.

Catilyn had been the woman's name, probably her parents had misspelled Caitlyn on the birth certificate. One day on a wellness check the woman had just broken down, and it had all come flooding out. The guy had been threatening to steal the very five-year-old girl Patty had been there to check on. What he had been planning to do with that kid didn't bear thinking about. Once Patty heard the woman's tale of woe, she offered to see if she couldn't get emergency shelter for the girl. What she also did was pump Catilyn for every detail she knew about the guy, his comings, his goings, everything.

Since then, she and Bentley had been scouting his place. Watching who came, who went, and more importantly when their target came and went. He had a little row home in a run-down part of town. The kind of neighborhood where even the good hard-working citizens who couldn't afford better, who were the majority of the population, knew to mind their own damned business if they wanted to keep having business to mind. His place was not run down, it had bars over the windows, but a nice hardwood front door. They had no doubt it was deadbolted more than once inside. The backyard was neat and well-kept as well. The place was the nicest-looking house in the neighborhood, which said a lot about the wages of sin.

Bentley had a plan to get them in the door. Once inside the rest should go easily. According to Catilyn, later in the evening the guy, whose name was Hunter, would start to sample his own products along with quite a bit of alcohol of some kind or the other. If you caught him early, he was sharp and tight, but right before closing up shop, he'd get bored with the diminishing clientele and chemically alleviate that unrest. Every one of these dealers always swore you didn't get high on your own supply, but sooner or later temptation would win a battle that wasn't even being fought that hard.

They saw their first target for their plan leave the house and start walking quickly in the direction of the subway a few blocks away. They put the big SUV into gear and rolled slowly around the block. Putting it in park again, Patty hopped out and looked cautiously around the corner of the deli that hunkered nearby, closed for the night. After a moment she turned to Bentley and gave him the thumbs up.

Bentley pulled the Jeep a little further forward and pulled up to the stop sign just as Hunter's buyer was reaching the corner. Bentley was out of the driver's side door in an instant a gun looking like the dark threat of death in his hand. The buyer turned to run and almost ran directly into Patty who had slid out from her hiding place to come up behind him.

She put the barrel of her own gun under the guy's chin. "Would you like to live to tell people about his later?"

She never got his answer because Bentley hit the guy in the back of the head with a blackjack, the lead shot making a bean bag sound before the buyer slumped boneless to the ground.

They kept the guy tied up at their place overnight. He came to only after he was already down in the basement strapped down long enough to get stiff and cold. One look around at where he was made him let out what would have been a piercing scream without the gag placed in his mouth in anticipation of just this reaction. Bentley just ignored his muffled screams and pleading noises and went about double-checking, making sure he was secure. After searching him earlier, they'd found he'd really only scored enough for the night, but him coming right back to the dealer that same night would be suspicious. They waited until the next day before they went down to the basement together to talk to him.

Bentley leaned over him and watched the buyer's eyes get huge in terror. He had no idea why this was happening to him, all he knew was that he was somewhere he didn't know, with two people who he didn't know in a position he couldn't explain. The only thing riding toward the positive was that they had so far done nothing to injure him. Except for knocking him out to get him here, but even in his panicked state, he could acknowledge that you needed to break a few eggs. It was still pretty reasonable to think that nothing good was coming next, no one knocks you out for anything good.

"All right, I'm going to take out the gag to talk to you. But I want you to know something, we're not interested in you, we're interested in getting inside Hunter's house. Now since Hunter isn't keen on letting people in that he doesn't know, that's where you come in. Do you call him or text to set up a deal?" Bentley asked before yanking out the buyer's gag.

"What? I-...."

"OK, let's start easier," Patty said. "Do you have a name?"

"Huh? Oh, my name's Sam, it's short for Samwise, my folks were big into the Lord of the Rings and stuff," the wide-eyed young man blurted.

Patty sighed a little at the additional unwanted information, but soldiered on, "All right Sam. We don't want to hurt you, well, no more than you've already been hurt to get you here. You are a way for us to achieve a goal, and that is to get into Hunter's place."

"But why? I mean....is it drugs or something? There's got to be an easier way than this," Sam was trying to think on the fly, trying to make all of whatever they had planned seem like a bad idea, so maybe they wouldn't need him anymore.

Patty let out a bitter little laugh, "Hardly. We need to prevent Hunter from doing something Hunter wants to do. See, a woman with a little girl is deep in debt to Hunter. Now, how much do you think films starring that little girl and all kinds of other people would go for on the dark web?"

Sam, to his credit, looked horrified at the thought of it. His first reaction was to say no way, no way would Hunter do something like that. Then he bit it back and rolled it over in his head. The guy was his drug dealer, how well did he even know him after that? He was always nice to Sam, but Sam was always a cash upfront sort of buyer, he could afford to be nice to Sam. In fact, he wanted to be nice to Sam to keep Sam coming back. He thought about Hunter's face, did he really think that face could go that dark if there was money owed? The more he thought about it, the more he didn't see why it wouldn't, that was the world Hunter lived in, and letting people ride on debts didn't look good. You become one person's soft touch; everybody would be reaching out their hands for you.

Sam quietly said, "Ok."

Patty gave him a smile, "Good guy. What do you do? Do you text him or call him when you want to make a buy?"

"I just text before I head over, and then text from outside," Sam explained.

"Does he have any security cameras? Guns that he brings to the door when he opens up?"

"Naw, he's not big time enough for that. I mean for cameras. He has quite a few guns, but I've bought enough times he doesn't bring them out into the open up for me," Sam shrugged.

"Perfect, warm those fingers up," Bentley said.

Chapter 7

Bentley had taken his place by the side of the door. He nodded over to Patty.

"All right there Sam, we're good to go. Text away," she said.

Sam sent the text poking at his screen with shaking fingers not being able to believe what he was doing. After hitting send he was left standing there on the stoop of the house looking forlorn. His emotions were a tangled mix of fear and other things that were harder to pin down. He felt like he was betraying Hunter, but deep down he knew, hearing what Hunter had planned to do, Sam felt like he'd be betraying himself if he didn't help these people put a stop to it. Of course, he only had their word for it, but on the other hand, they could have killed him already, and might still if he didn't do as they asked.

They heard Hunter's footsteps a moment before the bolts slid open and the door began to swing. It all happened so fast after that. The second the door began to pull inward Bentley kicked it the rest of the way open. Hunter slammed into the wall with a crash, thrown by the force of the door hitting him. Before he could even think to cry out, Bentley had the gun in his face.

Bentley slammed the door behind himself. Sam stood there; his mouth open in shock at what he'd just been a part of. He just liked to get high, that was it.

Sometimes you dealt with people you didn't trust to do that, but normally all you worried about was getting ripped off. But thanks to his pastime he'd inadvertently landed himself in the middle of some kind of high-stakes cop show drama.

He was about to crack a joke about just that to Patty when she said quietly from behind him, "Night nighttime."

Sam felt something jab into his neck. He turned to look at Patty as she was already pulling her hand away, her fingers almost daintily holding a needle. His face barely had time to register betrayal before his legs gave out from under him.

Patty and Bentley had an embarrassment of riches to deal with. On the floor of the fun room were two trussed-up and unconscious captives. It had never happened before, and frankly, the floor had become a little crowded. The unspoken agreement between them was that maybe it would be for the best if it never happened again.

"So, the plan is to keep Hunter as our pet, right?" Patty asked.

"Yeah, but now that we have both of them here, I can't help but wonder. Would old Samwise down there be the easier one to train? He seemed more tractable by nature, more open to suggestion," Bentley replied.

"Tell you what, let's table that and get started. We

can think on it while we cut their clothes off," Patty said.

"Why?"

"Look, even if we're using the one, we keep as nothing but a sex puppet, well, nobody buys a tiny dildo or a misshapen sex doll. We might as well get a look at the merchandise is what I'm saying," Patty said with an evil smile.

"True, if one of them has moles or something all over his ass, well we know who just gets killed and cooked, huh?" Bentley agreed wholeheartedly after only a moment's thought.

They both used scalpels and scissors working quickly to hack the clothes away. Soon the clothing from both men was nothing but a pathetic pile of rags that piled up next to their naked bodies. Unfortunately, the view did not make their decision easier for them. You wouldn't have known it to look at them, not by the way they carried themselves and acted, but both men had similar builds right down to decent-sized packages. Both were lean muscle all over, Hunter maybe a little darker in skin tone, but even that was negligible.

"Well, that didn't help," Bentley said forlornly.

"Let's keep Hunter," Patty said emphatically.

"Any reason why? Because I don't see a difference."

"I was thinking about it. I want to break that fucker all the way down to a simpering child. A drone with the audacity to suggest doing what he wanted to do....

that's some undeserved arrogance," Patty said flatly, clearly, she'd been thinking about it while they were undressing their captives.

"Well, that's fair enough. I can see that, a lot of pride and assumed power for a drone. Yeah, all right, let's get him on the table and get him through surgery number one," Bentley said.

"And hey, after this first one, he'll never see the other ones coming," Patty chuckled.

Hunter woke up. The world seemed out of sorts; he could barely think, his head was a complete fog. He didn't know where he was, nothing seemed on keel. He went to reach up to scratch at his eyes, something was in there, it hurt like hell. It took him a long moment to realize he couldn't move his arm. He tried to sit up, with similarly disheartening results.

"Hello?" he croaked without thinking. He kept trying to open his eyes, but they just would not open. What in the hell had happened to him? He tried to move his eyeballs to maybe unstick his eyelids. He kept trying, but nothing kept happening, he kept thinking about moving his eyes around, but nothing seemed to be responding, he couldn't feel that slight pain of muscle responding to his demands, nothing rolling around under his eyelids.

He paused, tried to wake up a little, and clear his head, which was hard, he was clearly on something. A memory returned, opening his door, the big guy... The big guy hitting him...

There was something specific about the pain in his eyelids, it was almost becoming clear to him. There was a series of sharp pains, both eyelids, both eyes. It was like...He tried to open his eyes again and felt a sharp tugging pain from his eyelids.

It was like.... his eyelids were sewn shut.

Hunter screamed.

Patty and Bentley had Sam strapped up onto the table. Bentley was considering how to position the various supports so they could enjoy Sam at optimum levels before they killed him. Patty already had the scalpel in her hand which she tapped impatiently against her hand. When Bentley finally locked in the struts, she moved over Samwise.

"You're going to reveal him while he's still unconscious?"

"No time like the present, the sooner this is done the sooner we can get to the fun stuff. Anyway, you like fucking them better once they're the faceless drone they've always been," Patty said, already holding up Sam's left ear like a prize for Bentley to see.

"True, and he's bonus material. We weren't counting on him," Bentley replied thoughtfully. There was a reproach buried in there that he hoped she wouldn't notice. Deep down he thought she was hoping to have Sam dead before he ever woke up. He could understand it, even if he didn't approve. He'd aided them willingly once he'd found out what kind of scum Hunter was. But in Bentley's mind, he'd helped the guy build the kind of mini empire where he felt he was safe stealing children. Every purchase the kid made from that guy had put more coin in the guy's purse. Sure, not all drug dealers were bad people by nature, but considering Hunter had the only nice house on his block, maybe Hunter counted as scum even before you knew about the child rape.

Not that it mattered, he considered as the other ear was thrown over his shoulder as Patty giggled, it was a minor point of contention. Maybe this drone was that naïve to not have seen his own crimes, more than enough of them were. Maybe she was right in making it easy for him.

"Get him hard for me," she said as she grabbed pliers to help her with his nose.

"Your wish is my command," he smiled as he went to load up a needle. "Reason you're doing the nose next?"

"Because I'm home free after this, the eyeballs are going to be easy, like scooping grapefruit after getting this off," she grunted as she struggled to get the nose to come free.

She wiped her brow as she tossed the nose aside once it had finally come free with a crack and a rush of blood. She grinned at Bentley holding up the spoon, "One scoop or two?"

"I think two would be a little less cruel at this point," he replied tossing the needle from injecting Sam into a wastebasket.

"Cruel to be kind?" she grinned moving toward the prone body with the tool they used.

Bentley chuckled as he began to remove his clothes. She was definitely in the spirit of things at this point, whatever doubts he had vanished in the wake of her cool efficiency. He dropped his pants first and kicked them behind them. His penis was hard as always and swayed and jiggled as he removed his shirt. He was impressed, by the time he had looked back, she had already deposited Sam's eyes carefully, stalks and all, onto the table they used for tools.

She winked, "Pull his feet toward the ceiling so you can get deeper, and let's party."

Bentley released the catches on the parts of the table that supported the legs. He ratcheted them up and away but kept the legs a little forward to make things better for Patty. By the time he was done, she had shed her own clothing and was climbing on top of Sam facing Bentley.

As he greased himself, she rubbed her open pussy lips back and forth on Sam's dick. She looked past her curls dropping in her face and kept her eyes locked on Bentley's the entire time as he stepped up and positioned himself and rubbed at Sam's puckered anus.

"Let's do it together baby," she breathed.

He nodded, "3"

"2." she gasped back at him.

"1," they said together before thrusting home.

Both must have been keyed up especially from the day's events because they used the faceless drone that thought his name was Sam with reckless abandon. The violence of Bentley's thrust had already caused blood to mix with the lube to create a pinkish sheen on his cock. Patty leaned forward for a moment and took Bentley's face in her hands and brought him close. As soon as he was within range, she locked her mouth to his, and her tongue plunged forward tangling with his as it thrust back at her stabbing and twirling. They both slowed for the moment, no longer considering the drone they were using, as in their hearts they only fucked each other as they kissed passionately.

Bentley pulled away a little from her, "We better finish soon, I think I'm going to cum soon."

"Try to wait for me baby," she said as she sped up her thrusting and twisting back onto Sam's cock, trying to find that magic angle and length to make it press on her g-spot.

He looked over her shoulder at the faceless one. He could see there had begun to be twitches in his cheeks and eyebrows. He'd be waking soon.

"It's about to get loud in here," he grunted as he

thrust inside.

She groaned in response, she'd found the perfect angle on his cock, and her orgasm was close on the horizon.

A moment later she grunted, "Tell me when you're ready."

A scream pierced the air as their victim came back to this world. The pain had finally found a way past the drugs, and enough consciousness had crept in for the totality of what had happened to become at least partially acknowledged.

Bentley practically had to yell, "Soon!"

She nodded and sat up just a little on the faceless one's penis. In her hand, she held a scalpel. "Say when baby."

"Now!" he groaned thrusting into the hilt.

She took the scalpel and dug it into the base of the cock that she held inside herself. She dragged it sharply and quickly around, including cutting the ball sack free of the torso. Bentley wouldn't have thought the screams from the drone could get louder, but now they were vocal cord destroying shattering in volume and shrillness. Blood spurted around her hand as she finished her work.

She thrust herself at an angle tearing the cock the rest of the way free from the body. Bentley watched her with rapture, like she was a goddess showing her aspect to him as she rose onto her knees. She smiled at him, rubbing her body, especially her tits with the dying man's blood. She took an already clotting glob and rubbed it vigorously into her clit. Her screams of passion overcame the screams of pain that were diminishing from the dying drone.

Her body froze, then it shook like she was freezing to death for a long moment. At last, she sighed and released the penis from her vagina allowing it to flop onto the almost deceased previous owner.

"And I thought you were going to go easy on him at first," Bentley grinned after he had pulled his shrinking cock out of the cooling sphincter.

"Naw, I was just drawing it out until he came to. I wanted music when I came, a sweet and faceless symphony."

"Well, one less thing to cut free when we gut him," Bentley laughed.

"I might keep it for a necklace," she laughed back at him.

Hunter was silent down in the basement, he had heard worse pain and fear than he felt in his own body and was considering the future.

They had just sent Hunter down into the sub-basement without ears and were entwined in the table device together. Patty dreamily ran her fingers through Bentley's chest hair, he reciprocated by running his own through her auburn locks.

"I had an idea recently," she said.

"Oh?"

"Just so you know this isn't half-cocked, I did some legwork on this, so please hear me out" she replied with a little trepidation creeping into her voice.

"In case you haven't noticed, I think you're relatively smart there," he chuckled. "I have every intention of hearing you out."

"We need, copycats."

"What? Why?"

"Because at the moment, we're starting to have to move more and more into stable people. The prostitutes and the junkies are being more careful. They can't prove anything of course, but they know we're out there. Having Hunter will take some of the pressure off us emotionally, but the work still needs to be done," she said causing Bentley to glow inside, she understood.

"All right, I can agree with that. But...."

"Again, hear me out. We, might be too smart to break into nice houses, or to leave a trail, but if we can inspire someone who is... Well, they'll get every missing person and murder anyone knows about hung on them when they get caught. It will buy us years, time we can use to get even more sophisticated, even more foolproof. We don't want this to ever end, we have work to do, we can't do it from jail," she explained.

"Yeah, I mean, I can see the logic there. Especially if we get a woman to go with Hunter, it buys us time to get better, but... nobody knows we're doing this, or why we're doing this. It's kind of hard to inspire copycats if they have nothing to copy," Bentley replied reasonably.

"We spell it out for them. Send a bit of spam to the right inboxes in the right places. There are mailing lists for everything these days. Write the kind of email that will inspire somebody, give them that final push. All it takes is one or two, let them operate a bit, let a few bodies get found, and wherever they operate gets all the views by the police. The rest of the city becomes open game for a while," she said.

"But they can trace stuff like that, hell, what ad company would even do it?"

"That is the beauty of the modern world, there's a Russian willing to do anything. And they're more or less impossible to trace. There's a whole dark web out there of goods and services my dear. It's amazing what you learn talking to kids these days," she grinned.

"Do you honestly think it will work? That the cops will heap it all on one guy? That someone will even get inspired by some email?" Bentley looked dubious.

"Dear, people have no idea how many mailing lists they're on. Some really, really suspect behavior is being scooped and sifted and categorized every time you accept cookies. Trust me, I anonymously mentioned on a site I know about that I wondered if data mining was capable of targeting ads to emails belonging to people who might be unstable. I got a lot of responses, all of them affirmative. " She smiled up at him, "All it takes is one person, better yet, a few in a couple of different cities, to get inspired. Once they're caught, look at what they did with Henry Lee Lucas, every sheriff in America showed up with their unsolved murders looking to get a confession. Suddenly every single missing person you and I had anything to do with goes away. All those missing persons reports will get filed and forgotten for good and always."

Bentley was silent for a long moment, "You think they could target the ads that specifically?"

"Yep, and it takes only one.... shall we say...respondent, and suddenly we're in the clear for a while," she smiled.

"How much will it cost?"

"A few thousand, I've checked around a bit. I've found a couple that have a reputation for being reliable, a few thousand in crypto, and poof, the money never happened, the transaction never happened, and the feds can't track shit except for 'somewhere in Russia' which can't be gotten to."

Hare barked at his screen, "Oh for the love of fuck!"

"What's up your ass," Burke demanded, looking up from his computer.

"Will you just come look at this? One of my little helpers in doper-ville sent me this. Said it looks like some kind of mass mailer...."

Burke took his time getting out of his chair. He generally took his time about everything in life. He viewed the world like this, in his line of work you might need to do a lot of rushing around in a hurry, it was best to be rested for when the time came.

"What's got your panties in a bunch?" he demanded as he came up behind Hare's seat.

"Look at this shit, there are some unhinged minds out there," Hare growled.

Burke read quietly out loud from a flashy screen with some kind of gory backdrop, "Look at the world you are forced to live in. How many people do you see that are all the same? They aren't people, they're categories. They're drones, they don't even deserve a face for all the personality they have. They take up space. They take up resources. Each one fits a stereotype, nay, revels and wallows in the safety of the stereotype. Imagine a world of real human beings, no longer forced to carry the drones...." He stopped reading. Finally, he said quietly, "If this was targeted to borderliners...How long until one of our little psychos sees this and finds their purpose in life?"

It took longer than they expected. It was three weeks before the first body showed up. As they stood there in the morning mist staring down at the mutilated corpse both Burke and Hare were sure it was related to the e-mail they'd seen. They had taped off the alleyway almost immediately and called forensics. They had uniforms trying to keep onlookers away until the meat wagon could get here and remove the victim.

Burke and Hare were so sure about the tie-in because the girl lying on her back in the alley had had her skin removed completely from the neck up. She had no face at all because, in her killer's mind, she hadn't deserved a face.

"Bingo!" Patty said happily.

"Huh?"

"Saw it in an email alert from the local news. We have our first taker of the bait!"

Bentley looked bemused, "What bait would that be?"

"Somebody killed after the ad. They found a body with no face at all," she said triumphantly.

"That's fucking awesome! Now could you give me those pliers so I can get the rest of his nose off?"

"We need a playmate; we've laid low too damned long. Not to mention, and I think it bears mentioning, with body two turning up, and where the hookers were grabbed, we know what districts have called in help to cover the streets," Patty announced.

Bentley smiled indulgently, as he would a child who couldn't wait to play a sport they were being taught, "Oh? And do you have somewhere in mind that isn't in that area?"

"I have better than that," she grinned. "I have culled a sheep from the herd outside of that area."

"Well, now I'm curious, do go on."

"She moved into the apartment building of one of my clients not too long ago. Out of town, farm girl type. She hasn't hooked yet, so cleaner than clean, but she's almost talked into it. One of the girls was bragging that any day now she'd be desperate enough. No family anywhere in the city, her vanishing shouldn't even raise an eyebrow."

"But have people seen you with her? Have you called her? That leaves records."

"I talk to a lot of the girls that live in those cheap places. I get tips that way, I can also find out if what my client is saying is what is. I only mentioned to her in passing that I might be able to find her work out here. Lack of money is why she's thinking about spreading them so I could tell she was all ears. Really, she's just like so many other cute little country girls that come to the big city and find out they aren't special and shit costs money. The whole thing is a cliché."

He nodded; Bentley had to admit he was intrigued by the possibilities. "The job thing?"

"I figured it might make good bait to get her to just come here easily on her own two feet. Laying groundwork," Patty smiled.

"Very devious, I take it you have a plan for that?"

"Very much so. I tell her since I can't be seen doing placement for somebody who isn't a client, she could meet me somewhere," Patty replied.

"Do you think she'll fall for it?"

Patty laughed, "Honey, the local girls almost have Little Holly Hobby convinced that it's fine to put a stranger's dick in her mouth for cash in the back of a car. Going on a ride to get some legit cleaning work with a social worker won't be hard."

Burke and Hare's life had become a plane of hell. They were up to three dead girls, but so far forensics hadn't given them anything yet that would help them nail whoever was doing this. Hare's biggest fear at this point, and one that he'd mentioned out loud, was what if the nutter just quit? Without enough to nail him now, if he just walked away, they'd never get him.

They'd had a shrink in and disclosed the pathology of the murders to him. Showed him the ad. The guy's helpful smile turned upside down immediately. He just started shaking his head.

"You say, you got this before you started getting bodies?"

Hare nodded.

"Yes, unfortunately, I see exactly what you want me to see. If there was someone out there already contemplating this path, or close to this path, this was probably the final little push they needed. Many of these people, they never act on it. They can never develop the kind of focus loci to finally get them over the hump, to finally give them the drive to take another life. This is like handing someone like that a pre-made pathology, ready for consumption," the shrink had said.

They'd sent him off to work out some kind of profile on their killer and told him they'd be in touch. The profile was nice, it narrowed things down a bit, they were looking at a younger, less molded psyche than their normal serial killer, probably in his twenties. By the time a guy starts up in his thirties, he usually has his own issues he's working through on the medium of human flesh. To be pushed over the edge like this, a guy would have had to have contemplated it, but not worked out enough of the why to finally do it. Hare had to face it, a loner in his twenties who spent a lot of time on a computer did not exactly narrow it down much in this day and age. Of course, the profile could be completely wrong, they didn't have a lot of experience with this kind of thing, and recent national events had proven older people weren't immune to a push over the edge.

So maybe they had a working profile, or maybe they had absolutely time-wasting garbage.

Which put them in the unfortunate position of having to wait until the perp fucked up somehow. And the mayor's office hated that answer, so they never gave it. Hare just smiled at them to their face, told them they were working some leads, and then laughed at the gullible fucks with Burke after he had gotten off the phone or out of the chief's office.

To make matters worse, he wasn't one hundred percent sure that this killer was the one responsible for the uptick in vanishings that were happening before they started finding bodies. It could be, God knew he wanted it to be. He supposed it was within the realm of possibility that this guy had been killing all along, and that email had just provided him with some kind of holy mission to justify his actions after the fact. But that didn't feel completely right. None of the bodies before had ever turned up. Those bodies that did turn up had been just normal hooking gone bad bodies, and this city was good for a set amount of those each and every year like clockwork. The people on his list had just vanished without any trace whatsoever, never to be heard from again. It didn't sound like this guy, this guy was just finding convenient patches out in the woods and leaving the bodies for the wild dogs. He was doing normal random hooker killings, but at an accelerated pace, and a huge twist on top.

And now, whatever had caused those disappearances was firmly on the back burner. There were no bodies to even prove those had been murder for one thing. Hell, they could possibly be the same perp if there even had been a murder. There were three in the morgue that had absolutely not died of natural causes, so that made it all hands-on deck, and interesting theories would have to wait.

154

Chapter 8

Ezra finally felt completely alive. Everything before this had just been going through the motions, killing time, waiting for something that would make it all make sense. He had things he wanted to do with his life, but he wasn't sure how, or even why, they were just all vague notions he acted on sometimes. One day, like magic, it had all fallen into place for him, and the world finally swam into focus completely. When he accidentally opened that email life made more sense than it ever had before. And it had been accidental, he'd meant to delete it but hit open instead. Once it had expanded on his computer screen the message's background had caught his eyes, but it was the words that had caught his soul.

He knew what needed doing, and who needed doing it to now.

This was what he'd been born for. He'd been so close that he could taste it before, but now it was right there where he could drink it all down and let it expand inside and fill him. Everything in life before now had just been useless directionless rage. He had always known that there were makers and takers, his life revolved around knowing that. He had known deep down some were born above others. But before he'd just been pissing in the wind thinking it had anything to do with race or religion or politics. No, it had everything to do with something deeper than that, the email had laid it all out for him, and he had understood it down to his bones.

The first time was terrifying, he had thought his heart would burst out of his chest. The stakes were so high to get this exactly right. The girl was doing a workmanlike job of pretending she liked it as he fucked her, and he was trying to pretend that it worked for him. And then it sank in, she was just another drone filling a role, her meter was running on this. They weren't experiencing anything that hadn't happened before, they were not having a human experience. And if she was gone, there would be another to take her place right under him. The thoughts had been bouncing back and forth in his head since the moment he'd read them, but now he understood. This wasn't a human being at all, its whole existence could be filled by a robot, and nobody would be able to tell the difference. It needed to end; real human beings needed to be ascendant again. And there was no time like the present he told himself as he began to choke the life out of her. It always took forever to kill with your bare hands, and he vowed not to do it like that again. Instead, he invested in stain-resistant vinyl seat covers. He just stabbed the next two when it was time to end the charade. Wipe away clean.

Tonight, it was time for number four. There was a special girl who wasn't very special at all, who was just waiting to make Ezra feel like the man, the human being he was always meant to be. He also knew he had to change hunting grounds some. The police were crawling over that little strip of cheap motels and hotels and abandoned buildings and bars he'd been hunting along. The girls were all working in packs with their cell phones handy as well. No, he needed to do something a bit different tonight.

The smart move now would be to really change things up, which was why he was headed for the suburbs. Tonight, he was going to try for a nice taste of "woman with only one car in the driveway." He'd scouted a bit during the week whenever he had time, checking off names, checking off Google searches, she had to be exact. Thanks to being observant as he crawled slowly by, he figured he had a good idea of whose precious hubby had a night shift, or worked late, who was single, etc. Ezra wasn't quite up for the full home invasion yet; men still had a tendency to worry him. But a little lady all alone, well, he had a big gun and ever so many knives.

He parked his truck well down the block in an area where people parked to go to a local recreation area where it could blend in. People always half-remembered a vehicle out of place. Maybe they didn't know they did, but if something jogged their memory it would come back to them. Like a truck parked right in front of a murder house for instance. People came up with a description of something like that.

Ezra had a route planned already. There was an alleyway behind the houses here, running along the oh-so-perfect picket fences that this little planned community loved so. He darted quickly through the yard of someone who lived down the street from his target. He'd noted before that they didn't have a dog, and there was never a car there at night. If all he wanted was to rob the place, he'd be in the right spot.

He had his gloves on before he eased their back gate open and skulked into the alley. It was neat and clean, this was not the kind of place where messes were tolerated, even back here away from prying public eyes. He kept to the abundant shadows whenever possible. Despite there being streetlights back here, they were spaced further out than out on the street out front creating deep pools of eternity. The only time he was forced out of the shadows was when he had to go by a house where he knew they had a dog and he needed to get away from the fence line. Just his luck the whole thing would be blown by somebody letting their yapping mongrel out for a late-night piddle.

This was the moment of truth when he moved on from the easy pickings to the real meat. He just needed to work the gate open, because it was all that stood between him and his chosen drone. He was breathing hard as he reached for it, not for any reason of exertion, Ezra had barely done anything yet. No, he was breathing hard because this was a threshold moment, and he knew it. All his other victims had been targets of ease and convenience. Hookers got right into your car; they expected you to fuck them, it was their role. They might not have expected what came next, but they were already where you wanted them. Not tonight, tonight he'd be springing a hell of a surprise on one lucky gal.

Tonight, he was going to kill someone he had watched, who he had handpicked and marked for sacrifice for the greater good. She was a drone of a human, everything about her was nothing. The tired divorced mom raising her little angel on her own. God, that was such a cliché of a life most authors wouldn't even touch it anymore, even movies avoided it. Yet here she was, sitting in the house she'd got in the divorce (Ezra would bet anything the husband had cheated) living this nothing of an existence as if it mattered to anyone. In reality, it only mattered to one person, it mattered to Ezra. And even then, it only mattered because he was clearing some dead space from the world, and she was the dead space. She was to be his first major deletion from the screen, and if it wasn't for that she would have nothing.

He wasn't picking up scraps tonight, bodies society was perfectly happy to be rid of and wouldn't miss. No, Heather Madison was a model little citizen. She belonged to a church, she showed up for parent-teacher conferences, she worked in management at a local call center. She counted in this world of ours as a good productive little cog in the wheel. As far as Ezra was concerned, there wasn't one single thing he could find out about her that was in any way unique or interesting. He'd looked at her Facebook page and her Instagram page, lots of posed shots, with fake smiles, surrounded by other drones giving the exact same smile.

If he was really serious about removing drones from the world, if he truly wanted to follow the message that was delivered to him, where he was standing was exactly where he needed to be. This was the source of banality itself.

He carefully and quietly worked a screwdriver in between the slats to get the latch that locked the gate. Once the screwdriver found the right spot, it flipped open and slid back easily, it was no more a lock than Heather was a person. In a matter of moments, he was in the gloom of her backyard looking at her house. No turning back now.

Ezra stood there for just a moment, taking deep breaths of oxygen, breathing in moments along with air. Not much further now, not much further at all. Soon, there would be one less of them sucking up the precious oxygen in the world. Her demise would free up the house for an actual human being. You'd have to be someone unique to still want the house after what would happen in there tonight.

First thing was first, little Mason was not allowed to be a bother to anyone for the rest of the night. The kid would have to be dealt with. Ezra made his way carefully first through the sliding glass door the kid left cracked every night, then up the stairs, keeping an eye peeled for any kind of camera light. Nothing. She hadn't realized she no longer had that safe hubby to make it his job to secure the home front for her. A lot of women get divorced, they put in security cameras, they buy a dog. Thankfully for tonight's entertainment, Heather had still felt secure in her little suburban wasteland. Must have been an amicable breakup.

On the landing and looking down the darkened upstairs hallway he already knew which door would be Mason's. The master bedroom would be down at the end, he could see the bathroom to his right, which meant door number three held visions of sugar plums dancing in a tiny head. Heather was the main course for tonight, but that was all in good time, he still had to start with the hors d'oeuvre.

The door opened smoothly and quietly, gliding across a thick rug. God bless newer construction they always want things muffled and whisper soft to match the future occupants. The room was illuminated by a soft night light by the bed creating especially deep shadows and giving off orange hints at the outskirts of the tiny light's range Posters of toys, and drawings Mason had probably done in class covered the walls. A little desk was on the left-hand side of the room, a cup full of pencils, and one of the large Crayola boxes sat on top, all training to be a future industrious worker bee. Next to that was an oversize toy bin, brimming with various trucks, cars, and other toys. Under the window was a low bookcase that was wedged with books. Ezra was a little surprised there wasn't a TV in here, it didn't fit the rest of the scene. Single mom, the easiest pacifier would be a game system in the room to buy her some time to think or drink. He had no doubt there was one downstairs but having it up here would free up the TV for Mom to swirl wine in front of.

Snuggled up to a large stuffed dog was the little man himself. The boy had pushed the covers down a bit, exposing pajama-clad arms and chest. The pajamas he was wearing must be a little warm even with the AC running lightly. In the gleam of the nightlight, Ezra could see a few little beads of sweat on the forehead that was framed by the tousled brown hair. The pajamas themselves presented smiling animated characters who had saved the universe on screen, they were oh so useless here.

Ezra took two steps, and he was by the bed, looking down at the idyllic scene of slumber. He reached down slowly, there was a flash of steel in his hand. Carefully, oh so carefully, Ezra reached out with one gloved hand and let it hover over the back of the boy's head. Finally, sure of his positioning, in one motion he pulled forward violently on the boy's head as he stabbed the blade directly under the skull and through the spine. The blade sank deep, and the boy's eyes shot open. The mouth flexed open and shut briefly as the child tried to scream. Ezra yanked his blade free allowing blood to begin to darken the boy's pillow like the tide on a dry beach. Mason tried to look around, but he was unable to turn and see who and what was the cause of this sudden nightmare he was experiencing. A little sigh escaped the button lips, which never passed air again. In only a few moments the boy had gone from being woken by a sharp stab of pain, to never feeling pain again.

Ezra left the boy's eyes open for the detectives to see later and left the room. He wanted those eyes to be accusing in the daylight, why didn't you prevent this? Mason was already drifting away in his mind once he reached the hall. It had been an enjoyable aperitif, but that was all Mason had been to Ezra. With any luck, those eyes would haunt the cops forever.

He had no idea what kind of man the boy would have become, though Ezra certainly had his suspicions. No, Mason was an obstacle to the real goal of the evening, a possible interruption to the night's entertainment if allowed to live. While Ezra couldn't admit to himself that he'd enjoyed killing the boy, at least one small little bit of him could acknowledge that it was always a moment of pleasure to step away from the constraints of society. He refused to let it bother him, it had been a businesslike affair without real deep passion. Maybe it bothered him to a degree as well because the kid hadn't had a chance to seal his fate yet. It didn't matter. It was in service of the mission, but it wasn't the mission. He moved on, he needed the mission, he needed the passion.

He was saving that passion for Heather, who was just lying there behind the door he stood in front of, unaware of the total changes happening to her little universe. Completely unable to stop them from happening, all of the control she had thought she had created for herself was already wiped away in the wash of her son's blood.

Her door slid open as soundlessly as the boy's had. Enough light filtered through her large window that Ezra could see her clearly on her bed. Ezra's breath caught at the sight of her. It wasn't beauty he saw, even if she wasn't unattractive, it still wasn't what held him so raptly. It was who she was, or more importantly, who she wasn't. She wasn't anyone interesting, she had no great goals, no anything but existing in the time-worn rut others had carved for her. And tonight, it would all change for her. Briefly, her life would have meaning and value finally, if only to Ezra.

He smiled, she was lying on her back breathing softly, nude, the sheet had been partially tossed off at some point. Maybe she no longer slept as soundly without the ex in the bed and tossed a bit before she settled in. Exposed like this, it was like she was a willing sacrifice for all this additional ease she was giving him in his goal. Just a large, razor-sharp blade against her throat like so. His hand on her forehead like so, and the blade forced viciously down and across like so.

Her eyes snapped open to see him smiling at her. She wanted to scream; she wanted to scream so badly her eyes registered confusion when she couldn't. Her arms flailed up, not at him, just some comical warding motion trying to make the whole bewildering world go away. Ezra couldn't help it; he began to chuckle at the sight of her as he watched her futile efforts to pull herself up from drowning in the middle of a nor'easter deep out to sea.

"Don't worry Heather, that pain will pass," Ezra said softly.

She looked at him with wild eyes, as if seeing him for the first time. The gash in her throat kept fluttering, the skin opening like a flower, as she desperately tried to suck in oxygen that would never come. Every gasping attempt only serving to bring drowning blood into her lungs. This was what he wanted, he wanted to watch the light begin to go out before he started his great work. He wanted her to have time to examine her life, to see and know what little it had all amounted to.

"I killed Mason first," he whispered.

She was already fading, but he could see the horror in those dimming eyes, and he relished it.

Now he could get to his real work, his statement.

He took out a series of blades, carefully laying them out on her nightstand. Then, he removed his clothing. He didn't have far to go to get to his ride, but covered in blood was no way to get there. Even the dimmest drone would notice that. She was almost gone when he made his first cut, slowly bringing a scalpel around her neck where it joined her chin and moving down a little to just below her hairline in the back.

When he made his next cut below her chin, joining it with the first, he was sure that if he had felt for a pulse there would have been none. Removing all the skin and hair on a head was painstaking work. You didn't want to damage or mar the skin more than you had to remove it, but you were still cutting something. He had botched it some the first time, his cuts had been jagged, the removal sloppy. But Ezra was an intelligent man, and willing to learn from his mistakes. He had invested in a flensing knife and spent some time with various YouTube videos learning how taxidermists worked. He had to give himself credit, he got better every time.

Ezra paused in his methodical cutting to take out a spoon and remove the eyeballs which he placed carefully in a jar of fluid he had in his bag of wonders. They got in the way as he worked to remove the skin. Not only did he have a technical reason for removing them, they made an interesting trophy in their own right. Once her eyes were peering at the inside of his bag, it was back to work. Painstakingly he would cut only where he felt he needed to, and separate skin from muscle the rest of the time by hand. It was painstaking careful work he was sweating even in this air conditioning before he was ready for the coup de grace. Carefully putting his fingers under the slits in her throat, he systematically eased her skin away from her head. The light gleamed off the red muscle and blood as it became exposed to the open air. For the first time in her life, she was perfect, exactly as she was meant to be.

As he placed her skin into a bag of salt he sighed with satisfaction. Now, now to his eyes, she looked like the glorious piece of art she had never been in life. He had never had his way with one of them after death, only as a way to prepare them, to get them in position beforehand for their demise. Looking at her, and seeing her like this, he felt his cock rise at the beauty deferred until death she had finally achieved. He had not articulated the idea before coming here consciously, but he couldn't help but note, even as he reached for his bag, that he had made a point of bringing a condom.

Ezra considered her positioning for a moment. He could use her any way he wanted; she certainly wouldn't complain at this point. He smiled, even with all of those options available, he still wanted her in missionary. That way he had the best view of her true face, the face that only he had been able to reveal to the world. He got onto the bed between her legs and slid the condom on, his grin widening as he shifted himself into position.

He couldn't help but laugh at himself, him pretending to himself he didn't know how this would end, there was even lube in the bag as well. Ezra had known damned well what he was going to do after Heather had died, yet he had refused to put it honestly to himself once. It had been cowardice on his part, a vestige of a society's rule book he'd already left far behind. Really, when he looked at it like that, Ezra couldn't help but laugh at it. He needed to be more brave, more honest with himself at least, especially since he could tell no one else. Maybe the drones couldn't see the majesty of what he was about and needed to be kept out of the loop, but the least he could do was be honest with the person who understood best, himself. He had always planned to fuck the newly freed of her false trappings Heather, next time he wouldn't bother to think he'd do otherwise.

Once in position he began carefully moving his cock about until the lube worked its way inside her. It was a different sensation altogether. There was no clutching heat and moisture to greet him as he entered her. The cooling flesh did not react to him, it didn't tell him what it desired, it desired nothing but the cold dirt of the grave. It was also so much better than he could believe. Ezra had seen the drone for what it was, had freed it of its mask, and in doing so he had made himself its master. It only reacted to his prodding at a mathematical level of force=action; it now knew its place. No interrupting the needs of real humans with the whining demands of the drone. No, now it existed as it always should have, as only a vessel for his pleasure.

Without thinking he kissed the spot where the lips had been, mashing his mouth against the bloody teeth. Ezra caught himself and yanked his mouth back. Saliva could be traced; he'd need to wipe her teeth off when he was finished. His purloined kiss wouldn't have long to contaminate the scene, he'd be finished soon, and he had her blood on his lips to taste while he reached his peak.

Withdrawing was sorrow, but he had to leave soon and he still had things to do.

Quickly he went to the attached bathroom and rinsed the blood off of himself. Then he returned to the bed. He ripped open an alcohol swab, and vigorously wiped down the area around her mouth and her teeth causing them to gleam. Next was an inspection of the sheet directly below her, and her vaginal area. He was looking for his own curly pubes sticking out anywhere. After tonight, he resigned himself to shaving, he knew he'd make passionate love to the next one too.

Satisfied that the crime scene was useless to the police, he got dressed. Finally, he took out his digital camera and a tripod. He needed the tripod because he didn't dare risk a flash. He needed to take long exposures to capture her glory. Ezra propped her head up on a pillow carefully, then set up the tripod at the edge of the bed. This way he could get not only her glorious transformation, but he could also get her gaping, recently used pussy in the shot. These images would get him through the lean times, while he culled his next victim out of the herd.

Satisfied, he carefully refilled his backpack. He looked over the room taking in every detail to savor it, and to make sure he hadn't left some accidental detail for the police. He gave the place one last glance before he left the way he had come, leaving devastation, or art, in his wake.

"What took you so fucking long?" Burke demanded as Hare got out of his car.

"I was out when the call came in. It took them a while to think to just fucking text me," Hare said.

"Well come on in, forensics are working it, but I think you have to see this to really believe it," Burke growled as he turned around to re-enter the house.

"How many dbs?"

"Just two, one Heather Madison, and her son Mason."

"They pick up a husband or boyfriend yet?" Hare asked.

Burke sighed and then started walking up the stairs, "Yeah, we have the ex-husband in for questioning. Sounds like he's got an alibi, worse, it was an amicable divorce. But I don't think it would matter if he didn't."

"Why not?" Hare demanded as they came up to an open door at the end of the hallway, where he could see somebody from forensics taking photographs.

"See for yourself," Burke moved out of the way with an expansive wave of his arm, like a maître d'hôtel welcoming a special guest to a private party.

Hare stepped through the door and froze. Heather Madison's ghastly skinless face greeted him. It could not be said to be staring at him, you needed eyes for that. Its expression was only dry and crusting blood.

"Dear Lord," he breathed.

"This looks like our new buddy, don't it?" Burke said coming up on Hare's shoulder as he stood in the doorway.

"Yeah, unless it's a copycat, which I doubt, it's too early," Hare replied quietly.

"For fuck's sake, he's killing real people now! He kills junkies and whores, the major's office only cares about it being in the papers and on TV, he starts killing off suburban moms… If we don't get tossed off this case altogether, I hope you like the fucking words 'task force' because you're about to hear them," Burke snarled. His annoyance was understandable, Burke didn't work well with others. He barely tolerated Hare some days, and they had worked together for over a decade, more closely than anyone else Burke had ever worked with.

Having a bunch of detectives thinking they could bother him at his desk must be burning his ass.

"Whatever," shrugged Hare in response.

"Whatever? You seem pretty mellow about this, and you smelled it coming before anyone. Hell, you think this guy is behind your disappearances from before?"

Hare nodded, "He could be, that email might have given him the idea to change his m/o, to want to make some kind of fucked up statement. Yeah, I don't care if we have to do a task force Bill, I really don't."

"And why is that?"

"I just want to get this fucker the fuck off the streets so I never, ever have to see something like this again as long as I live," Hare replied.

"I got more bad news."

"Oh goody, might as well as get it all over with now, so we can wander around hoping we find a sign saying, 'I did it, this is my address' because so far this guy has left us fuck all."

"Similar m/o in a case in Miami, and two in Los Angeles," Burke said quietly.

"So, how long until we're working in conjunction with the feds on this?"

"You want it down to hours and minutes? Because I assume there's already been calls made," Burke replied.

"Oh, fucking goody some more, that will put the

cherry on my sundae."

Ezra parked his truck in his driveway after leaving his pleasures behind. Going in the garage side door he quickly opened a beer as he sat down in the well-lit and tidy garage and pounded it. A little stink of booze, and really, that's all Sasha needed to put her mind at ease as to what he'd been doing. In a great big way, smoking being banned in bars did him a huge favor. Getting the smell of cigarette smoke into your clothes must have been a real bitch back in the day.

Sasha was already asleep, but when she woke up tomorrow if she caught a whiff of beer on him and no perfume, she'd be perfectly happy to believe he'd been at the bar with his buddies. He barely had any friends, but it made her happy to think he did, so that was what he told her. He used to go for militia weekends but had given up on them deciding they were posers. Ezra didn't go out often, so she didn't mind losing him to his buddies once or twice a week. He was always perfectly attentive the next day, including in the martial arts, so she had no reason to think that anything was occurring other than pool and beer.

He quickly downed another one, put both of them into the recycling before he went in. Instead of heading for the bedroom, he headed for the basement. The basement was completely furnished, and a nice place to watch a game or a movie in one of the easy chairs down there. There was one door that led from the main room you could see, and two you couldn't see. Putting them in had been hard work, and not cheap, but that's why you had a nice job. So, you could treat yourself.

Sasha was not allowed in either space, no one was. The first was for when society finally hit a wall and crumbled, she knew about that, but it wasn't her place to disturb it. Either one of two things would happen, either the takers would finally get it in their heads to start taking even more, or the damned government would finally just get bought out by the damned Chinese communists. Either way, Ezra was prepared to make sure he and Sasha survived it. That door had a combination lock that only he knew, inside was food, guns, beds, and water. A place to hide while the drones burnt the world to the ground. The other door...it didn't lead to a big room, maybe ten by ten, Sasha didn't even know about its existence.

Inside were the things the rest of the world, Sasha included, didn't need to know about yet. The things that meant the most to Ezra, the ones he dreamed about each night. Little mementos from before he found his real purpose in life dominated the collection. Just women he'd killed over the years to keep himself from snapping in public. A way to take the edge off, he'd discovered that he could function perfectly in this sick and fucked up society if every once in a while, someone died, and he could look at them while they did. He could conjure up that memory in his mind's eye for years, and it would be enough for when the bitch wanted to redecorate, or one of his wetbacks got deported from one of his restaurants. He could just conjure up that image... and all the rage went away. If he kept something, well, the image would last longer.

But that was spread over years and years. Before he had gotten a purpose.

But that was before. He laughed at that man, all that rage, all that disgust at what society had become just flailing endlessly at shadows. Here was progress. On the shelves, he had the racks of dummy heads he'd found in a dumpster at a department store that had been on its way to become his newest eatery. Sasha went to visit her parents, and he'd brought them down here. At the time he hadn't known what he wanted them for, something had just told him he'd find a use for them.

How right he had been.

Carefully, almost reverentially, he removed the heavily salted face of one of the hookers from a bag it had been carefully wrapped in. Heather wouldn't be ready for display for a few days. Tanning was a process. But the hooker was done with the first step, and he carefully laid the salted hood of flesh over the mannequin's head. This would help get the wrinkles out. At this point, he could frankly leave it like that for months before he did the final steps.

But if he wanted forever, well, the next step was

pickling. He was slowly getting the chemicals he needed down here for that. No hurry, he had plenty of heads to put those faces onto that the drones had stolen and went around thinking they deserved. And really, it gave him pleasure to take a moment to spend time with his ladies.

Chapter 9

Carol sat alone at a bus station. It wasn't the big city hub with loads of buses and people moving like the swirl of a hive, just a regional for people going to the burbs. She had chosen to sit outside to hopefully be easy to find away from what noise and crowds there were. She was beginning to feel like an idiot as she sat there watching people come and go. All their movements showed the direction and purpose her life sorely lacked. The social worker woman had said she'd take her out to the guy who needed cleaning if she had time today. It wasn't written in stone that they were going, Carol had just wanted to believe it was. Like the ever-hopeful fool she knew she was, here she had been twenty minutes early. Sitting there in her nicest clothes while trying to not look appealing to the various men, and some women who prowled the streets and the bus and train stations for meat, even in the daytime.

She had gotten even more nervous about possibly getting approached after the most recent bus had come and gone. Carol worried that someone might have seen her ignore the bus and wonder if she was there for something more fun. But the thing was, she had to stick it out, she needed this job. She had to have it, or she just might very well end up at a bus stop either leaving the city to go back to her humiliation at home or waiting for a passerby who wanted to have that kind of fun for money. She had work, but it was part-time at a grocery store, and as was she had to skimp on food some days just to make sure she had the rent paid in full. And that was with the employee discount at the place she worked at supplementing her meager income.

She had reached a point where either she needed to do better financially, or she'd have to admit she'd failed. Her savings were almost gone, she'd have to go back to living at the farm with John, crawling back like a whipped dog who couldn't hack the real world. John wasn't the problem.... well, no, in many ways he was. He was protective, he wanted to make the world an easier place for her after their parents had died. But if he protected her as much as he wanted, she'd have no life whatsoever. And when she'd tried to have a social life back home.... the end result had been her running to the city to get away from the consequences. Including John, John had become a consequence as well. It had all come down to today, to getting a better job. Whether that job was cleaning a guy's house or letting one get his business done on her bare skin was still up in the air.

Just when she was beginning to think she had been stood up an SUV pulled up. The social worker woman was driving it. Thank God.

The window came down and Patty shouted, "Quick, hop in, I can't really stop here!"

Already cars behind the SUV were honking as Carol dove for the door, The irate world went away the second the door shut on the climate-controlled environment, and the other woman pulled away. They were now enveloped in a cocoon protecting them from the discomfort of the hostile world.

"Sorry, I was a little late," Patty said with a smile as she pulled into traffic. "It never ends some days, it really doesn't."

"The guy isn't going to mind a bit of tardiness, is he?" Carol asked nervously.

"No, no, I'm doing him a favor as much as I'm doing you one. Maybe more so. You ever try to find the exact right person for a position? I mean someone you want to leave unattended in your house?"

Carol blushed a little before she said, "No, I can't say as it's ever come up."

"It can be a nightmare, lot of weirdos out there in this big world."

Carol nodded a little ruefully, memories of home coming up unbidden, "Yes, there certainly are. Even when you think you're safe."

The pair of them talked casually as they made their way out into the suburbs. A bit of where are you from, a bit of where do you like to eat, a lot of avoiding any topic anyone would be legitimately interested in. The further out from downtown they got, the more nervous Carol became. Finally, she asked the question that had begun to weigh on her mind, "How am I ever going to get out here?"

"Don't worry kiddo, it's only once a week, and there's a bus line that doesn't run far from the house, he doesn't mind picking up and dropping off from there. Hey, maybe you can save a bit from this, actually, get your own car."

"I doubt he pays that well."

Patty laughed, a throaty sound full of sincere humor, "Well, we all have to start somewhere. And like I told you before, he pays pretty well regardless."

"I'd be happy with a full refrigerator."

"Way to keep those expectations reasonable, if only my clients did," Patty laughed again.

They pulled into the driveway; Carol was a little taken aback by the appearance of the place. It didn't look so much *bad* as it looked poorly maintained, like a nice house gone to pot. The walls hadn't been pressure washed in years, nor had the gutter been cleaned judging by the plants she could see peeking out, and the grass has become a small savannah with only the thin trail of the walkway to break it up.

"I wonder if I could get in extra doing yard work," she mused.

"Probably, his problem is he's single and he works all the time. I had to help him clean up some and while we were doing it, I convinced him he should just hire somebody. It isn't like he can't afford it," Patty replied as they parked the car. "I warn you though, it is definitely still pretty messy in there. You'll be earning the paycheck."

They got out of the car and made their way up the overgrown concrete walkway to the house. Carol could see and appreciate the scenario Patty had just described. With her there their house back home had never gotten dirty, never even dusty, but John had never had the time for the niceties that brighten up a house's appearance. It just took more time than he had. Probably a similar soul, if it wasn't business, it didn't need doing. She wondered what their childhood home looked like now without her there.

Before they reached the front door it swung open to greet them. Standing there was a muscular man, going a little to pot, she could see the gut through his shirt. But he had chosen his shirt wisely to downplay his waist and to show off his shoulders. His hair was fashionably short, gray barely showed on his temples. Carol couldn't help but wonder if she was seeing some of Patty's handiwork extending to the man's wardrobe.

"Hi Patty, I take it this is.... crap I'm terrible with names..." the man said, a look of embarrassment coming over his face as he realized he had blanked on the name of his interviewee.

"Carol" Carol filled in.

"Carol! Great! Well, I guess Patty has already filled you in that I'm a slob due to work. The house has a furnished basement, so why don't we start there, and I'll give you the full tour top to bottom. Well, bottom to top really. I know it's probably going to seem a lot, both the size of the place, and the mess, but I promise you I'll pay well. Patty finally got it through my head that I make a little too much to be living like this, so I'm taking her advice," the man said in a warm and friendly tone.

"I twisted your arm hard enough," Patty laughed lightly.

The man laughed as well, before he held out his hand to Carol, "Forget my own head, I'm Bentley by the way."

She shook his hand, it was strong, with some callousing, but not nearly as much as John had on his.

"Shall we get started?" he asked.

"Let's, please," Carol said.

"Yeah, it would be a good idea if we could wrap this up so I can get Carol back into town, technically I'm on the clock here," Patty pointed out.

"If we go too long, I can always make the time to take her back," Bentley replied.

Bentley led the way inside, Carol followed right behind him, with Patty bringing up the rear. Carol was taken aback immediately by how messy the house was. She had been warned, but a verbal warning and what she was confronted with were two different things. This looked like the kind of place you saw with an obese or elderly shut-in on a TV show, it didn't jibe with the powerfully built urbane man in front of her.

"I warned you," Patty said, as she could see Carol's

head roving the house. "He basically comes in and makes a mess then leaves to go to work again."

"I'd like to deny that, but unfortunately the results are evident," Bentley said ruefully from the front.

He made his way through the house with the two women tailing him until he opened a door off to the side. Even if it was furnished, Carol could still feel the cool puff of air from underground as soon as the door opened. Bentley turned on the light and began down the steps. Carol was relieved to see that at least what the basement mainly suffered from dust and only a bit of disorder. Not only was she glad the full tour was starting down here, but she also vowed to get this cleaned first, just for the sense of accomplishment.

Bentley waved his arm expansively, "At least this shouldn't take long. Might as well show you where I keep the washer and dryer while we're here, you'll probably…no you'll definitely need it."

With that, he stepped through a door on the far side of the room without looking back. The next room was almost clean in appearance, even if the concrete finish made it seem a bit shabby. "Over there's the washer and dryer, you can give them a once over, see if you have any questions on how to operate them."

Carol dutifully stepped over to the units sitting almost forlornly in the empty, hard concrete room. The dryer was pretty self-explanatory, it wasn't that new or complicated. The washer seemed a bit on the newer side, the controls seemed pretty straightforward, but she was sure there'd be some getting used to it.

"If you could bring a load down you could walk..." Her words were cut off when Bentley's strong arms slid under hers, up and around, his hands clasped behind her head in an instant putting her in a full nelson before she could even register what was happening.

"Patty!" she yelled for help. Looking over, she died a little inside when she saw Patty ignoring Bentley grabbing her. Instead of rushing to her aid, her hoped-for savior was instead pulling at something in the wall. Carol froze a bit when she saw it was a door, and worse, the hidden tunnel the door revealed.

Terror caught her as she breathed, "Oh no....please God no, Patty, please.... please help me!"

Bentley chuckled as he pushed the petite woman in the direction of the opening, half dragging her as she tried futilely to resist his momentum, her pump coming off her foot as she kicked. "Don't know what you're asking Patty for help for, you were her suggestion."

Carol began to scream, her eyes snapped shut with terror. She stopped when she received a ringing slap to the face, the warmth spreading immediately where the hand had struck her.

Patty stood in front of her, her face looking stern as she shook her hand. "You can scream your fool head off my little country blossom, but trust me, ain't nobody on earth can hear you. So why don't you be a good girl for the time being, and we'll see where we are in a little while. Maybe you walk out of this with nothing more than a well-deserved lesson in city life."

Carol wanted to scream some more, but she could also see that Patty would love nothing more than to provide her with more abuse. Not to mention, other than flailing about with her legs, she was truly helpless. Bentley easily picked her up with the full nelson and dragged her forward. She could get no purchase to free herself no matter how she tried to squirm away from the big man.

She half stumbled and was half dragged along the short hallway, which ended in a concrete and cinderblock room. She took one look around the room, saw all the implements inside of it, and began to sob. Tears streamed down her face; her breath began to come in hard shuddering gasps that shook her whole body. She was so overwrought by what she had seen in that room she barely even registered the shift in position when they were in the next room.

Even then she hadn't even begun to take it in before she felt her legs being lifted upward, and Bentley himself hauled up on her from his end. She was set down on a bed of some kind, she looked down to see Patty already strapping her leg down. Carol tried to kick with the other one, but she missed Patty's head, and then suddenly a wave of pain rushed through her as Bentley applied an enormous amount of pressure on the full nelson causing her to gasp explosively. By the time she recovered, Patty was already pulling the strap tight on her other leg.

As Patty moved up and took an arm from Bentley to strap it above her head, Carol had been reduced to a litany of pleas to heaven. A repeated and mucus-filled, "Please...please God....please God no....please."

Bentley himself strapped the other arm up.

"Here you go Hun," Patty said, Carol could see she had handed him a pair of scissors, a matching set were in her other hand. Both of them began to cut off Carol's clothes, first, the dress she was wearing, her nicest one, then they began to work on her bra and panties.

"Why? Why are you doing this? I barely know you people, I've never done anything to you," Carol cried.

Patty leaned in, as Bentley continued the work of reducing her to nakedness. "See, but we know you, right down to your core. The thing is my girl, you haven't done anything to anyone. Nor will you. Nothing of any interest at any rate. What do you provide the world that thirty-five other girls just in this city don't do just as well, and just as generically as you? What is happening to you now is the closest to interesting, the closest to greatness as you'll ever come. Enjoy this moment, it's the most powerful in your entire life."

Carol could only stare at her with a lack of comprehension on her face as Patty pulled away. She heard her say to the man, "I'm going to guess lil Miss

Pearl Pureheart here is as dry as the Sahara right now, why don't you let me warm her up for you a bit? Get her nice and wet?"

Carol heard Bentley chuckle and deep throaty appreciative laugh, as Patty vanished from sight. There was a cranking on the table below her, and against her will her strapped-down legs were being spread wide until she was splayed and on display. Carol's skin had already begun to goose pimple, even though this room wasn't particularly cold. The feeling of chill that came over her meant that she jumped in her restraints a bit when she felt the other woman's warm breath on her inner thighs. Carol knew what was coming and was trying to find a way of getting her mind away from it, to put her thoughts anywhere else. The woman just kept breathing heavily the moist air trapping in that area. And then she felt the wet tongue touch her.

"Noooooo!" she screamed.

This caught Bentley's attention, he loomed over her, "Don't make my ears hurt, do it one more time and I'll put something in your mouth to quiet you!"

Carol tried to pull into herself, her own head became an echo chamber filled with her own voice repeating a mantra over and over of, "This isn't so bad, relax, this isn't so bad, there's nothing you can do, this isn't so bad." She tried to force herself to, if not enjoy the woman's ministrations, at least to try and turn the revulsion to some level of acceptance. It was that or shut down entirely, and some fight instinct wouldn't let her mind do that, it couldn't just cocoon itself away somewhere until this was over. God, that would be so good if she could, but no matter how hard she tried, the sensations coming from below told her that this was real, that was happening. Worse than anything imaginable, a set of her nerve endings were responding to it, she felt betrayed as she felt herself moisten.

"How's it going babe?" she heard the man say, breaking her concentration.

After a pause, Patty spit, "Sorry, cunt hair. Oh, she's wet, but I think I can make her even wetter."

"Go for it. Give her the works."

A moment later Carol screamed in pain, without warning she felt the woman's teeth clamp right through the sensitive flesh of her labia! Waves of sharp pain washed over her entire body. Over her own sobs, she could hear the woman spit a piece of flesh out. "It's better, but I can do better yet."

Carol was shocked when the woman started licking and teasing her clit, confusing her senses. Pleasure sensors were firing directly next to a source of sudden and extreme pain. Her head swam in confusion.

She heard a buzzing sound near her. A moment later she felt the first swipe of a set of clippers on her head. "No....not my hair.... please!" she begged as the long locks began to tumble off her head like wisps of spider's web falling from the sky.

The man laughed, "Bitch just lost a cunt lip, and she's crying about her hair. They care more about their disguise than they do their own body."

Carol could feel the woman chuckle around her clit, the breath pushing at the entrance to her vagina.

And then she screamed even louder, an animal sound that seemed to shake the room. The woman had latched her teeth onto Carol's clit, first slicing at it with her incisors, and then tugging at it with her outer molars. Carol had never felt pain in her life the way she did as the evil bitch below her clamped down and tugged. And then, just like that, most of her pleasure sensors left her poor abused womanhood.

Patty stood up with a smile, blood smeared down her face, and down onto her shirt. She walked over to Bentley and kissed him deeply, forcing the piece of flesh she'd torn from Carol into his mouth. He pulled back and smiled lovingly at Patty, chewing on what had once been Carol's clitoris, rolling it around his teeth like a piece of jerky he wanted to savor for a bit.

Patty smiled wickedly, "I think she's plenty wet now, why don't you fuck her, and I'll finish her while you watch?"

"Yeah, I could use to relieve some pressure in a warm wet place," he smirked moving down the table to where Carol's strapped-down legs were spread wide awaiting him.

Carol barely felt him enter her, there was so much

pain in the area it barely registered. His presence was there, she couldn't ignore the feeling of intrusion, but actual sensation at this point was overwhelmed by the other wounds she'd received.

"Don't get too frisky lover, I still have some adjustments to make up here before she's perfect," Patty winked at him as she turned to the tray Bentley had pulled to near the bed.

Before Carol even realized what was happening, she felt a sharp pain in the skin under her ear. It wasn't the violent pain that had happened to her before, and with the man banging his pelvis into those wounds this pain seemed cleaner in comparison. The sharpness hurt, but it was a lesser hurt. She was horrified a moment later when her ear flew over her face. Rape wasn't the sole intention here, if anything it seemed to be a side effect of what their real goal was, mutilation.

Patty leaned over Carol's face and smiled. In her hand, she held an object that looked like a small flat spoon on the end of a metal stick, "Care to guess what this little baby is for?"

Carol tried to shake her head as violently as she still had energy to do only to find padded plates holding her in place.

"It's called an evisceration spoon," Patty said. An instant later Patty's other hand clutched Carol's face and forced her eyelid back. Carol could see the spoon approaching, looming larger and larger in her vision until it was all she could see. She felt a sharp tugging pain, her vision shifted wildly, and then, there was no vision on that side anymore.

Patty shifted onto the other side of the bed, with the now bloody spoon still in her hand. She gasped with relief when Patty set it down and picked up something else. Carol felt the sharp pain again, this time on her other ear. It hurt, but there was so much pain in so many areas now, Carol felt only resignation to losing the second ear. She felt it coming away this time, as a piece of flesh hung for a second and Patty just tugged it free.

Patty's face reappeared, Carol tried to twist her head away. It earned her a ringing slap right where the ear used to be. Before she could recover her senses, her eyelid over her remaining eye was pried open. She saw the spoon approaching again. In so little time something so irreversible occurred, it was hard to even consider what had happened when the world blinked out and she was able to view nothing but blackness. Carol tried not to panic at the loss of light, her whole world had become a black void filled with nothing but painful inputs attacking her at every angle. Even her hearing was muddled with the lack of an ear to project sound inward and the blood clotting over the canal to the inner ear.

Carol was finally feeling a blissful separation from what was happening. Her body had suffered too much pain, far too quickly. Adding to her loss of reality, she had lost a significant amount of blood. She barely noticed when the cutting began around her nose. She didn't make a sound as the sharp fire traced along the sides of each nostril. She managed a whimper when the shot of pain came that told her it had been snapped completely off her face.

Some part of her was only sad, knowing that this was the end. Carol doubted she could even survive the wounds she'd suffered if someone began caring for her immediately. If Patty and Bentley got up and left the room, she'd die just as easily from what they'd already done as anything they still might do. As horribly mangled as she was, she doubted she'd want to live regardless. Whatever they did now would only hasten the process so in that light it could be viewed as a blessing.

She could hear Patty through the clots saying, "Tell me when you're ready baby."

"About to...." Bentley's voice came to Carol through cotton.

"Do it now!" he shouted, but to Carol, he sounded like he was in another room.

Carol felt a sharp pain in her chest, it took her breath away. She managed to gasp out two words.

"Sorry... John," she said as the world moved away from her. There was no panic or fear, secretly she was glad, the pains were ebbing away, it seemed that was what all the world had been in the end. Nothing but pain, regrets, and dim memories of happiness to ensure the pain hurt more.

Bentley pulled out of the body after a long moment where he had shuddered inside of it. They hadn't done a female drone in forever it seemed, he forgot how much he liked being inside one when they died. His face regaining composure, he looked up at Patty to find her grinning at him.

"What?" he demanded.

"You have the sweetest goofiest look on your face right after you cum really hard. I was just savoring the moment," she said.

"Well, so do you."

"Speaking of which, I'm all riled up, I think I'm going to see if our toy downstairs has made progress in being amenable to playtime."

"I think we need a female one too, sometimes I just don't feel like tearing up an ass," he said, with only the slightest twinge of jealousy. That was what they had the guy in a cage for, but still, Bentley was never good at sharing.

Patty laughed, "Put it on top of our to-do list. I mean, right after I see if the drone's ready to fuck or not."

John had to turn the tractor off and sit for a moment. If he was at all concerned about it anymore, he would have wished he had turned it off sooner. Before he had left it drift across three rows of corn. He didn't care, he didn't even care about the corn, it was just that the bumping and jarring of the vehicle as it hit each row got through to his brain enough for him to reach down unthinkingly and turn the key.

His sister was dead.

No one had told him, there were no phone calls, there didn't need to be. John could sense things, sometimes sharp and clear, sometimes as a vague feeling. He could sense when he walked next to a person who had done something really bad. Sometimes, if they left something behind, he could follow them with it, sometimes he didn't even need that. He didn't think of himself as psychic as much as he did a lucky guesser. The one constant in that weird noise in his head was the connection he had with his little sister. He could be two fields over and know when she had fallen out of a tree and hurt herself. He had no problem taking steps last year when that boy had interfered with her. Carol had had problems with the steps he had taken, and he felt that her guilt over it had caused her to leave home. He always suspected that she had hoped the distance would free her of what she felt was his constant looking over her shoulder and meddling in her life.

He hadn't meant to, but when she hurt, he hurt. He had to protect her.

And now, he couldn't protect her anymore. No one could protect her anymore.

She was dead.

He shook his head to clear it a little and started the tractor back up. He needed to go to the city to sort this out. He needed to know every detail of Carol's last moments, and he would deal accordingly with what he found out. But that meant he had to take action now before the waves of sadness crushed him under and pinned him in place like a butterfly in a collection.

He had the rest of his life to mourn, but he only had this moment to get to work. The tractor roared back to life, and slowly he forced it back to the long patches of grass between the fence line and the field that existed for traveling from spot to spot on the farm. Other farmers were using ATVs to do that kind of travel, but John still felt better about having the big workhorse of a tractor under him. Maybe it made him feel more like a serious farmer, and less like a kid at play. Maybe he just liked being high up and able to survey his world, his farm. It had been their farm before she'd left.

Chapter 10

Burke was sitting against his car eating a donut and staring out into space when Hare pulled to a stop.

Hare didn't even bother with formalities, "What the fuck now?"

Burke gestured with his donut, white powder coating his thick fingers as they aimed in the direction of a small copse of woods near an abandoned brick factory of some kind. "Go have a peek see, then you tell me."

Hare growled something under his breath and made his way toward where there was already tape strung between the trees. His feet crunched over broken glass and gravel; his legs dragged through tall weeds as he went. Hare passed close by the remains of the building, trying to keep something awful that was most likely hidden in the weeds from getting on his shoes. These places, once they lost humans, they became soaked in foul liquids it seemed, and covered in broken glass and other scattered refuse. Like the world put its mark on the place warning others to go there no longer, to tell man, "You left this place for a reason, go back."

Well, someone had at least stopped by.

Hare made his way to the corpse of woods where forensics were swarming around taking pictures and moved in as close as he could without worrying about evidence.

He whirled back toward Burke yelling in a tight voice, "Mother fucker!"

Burke waited until he came closer before saying, "Motherfucker is right. Want a donut?"

Hare shook his head no, "You think it's our boy or just a copycat?"

Burke shrugged, "Maybe the suburban thing was the copycat. Maybe it is our boy doing both town and country. Maybe he just did this one as a quick fix because hookers are an easy target until he can line up some more actual people anyone gives a shit about?"

"I wish you'd stop saying that real people shit. We got an ID yet?"

"Her wallet says Tamara Thornton. I knew her as TT from a vice sting, man she was a crazy piece of ass. Now here's where it gets dicey, different neighborhood than the previous hookers."

"Double fuck."

"With sprinkles on top. Wanna hear my theory?"

Hare sighed, "Go for it, I'd love to know. At least you got a fucking theory."

Burke leaned back, which pushed his stomach out past his sport coat, "I think the guy has been thinking about doing this for a long-damned time. Maybe even acted on it a few times, random thrill kills sort of thing. He's studied other freaks and saw where they got caught. He's shifting m/os a bit just to fuck us in the ass. Yeah, he's got his little trademark, but he's hitting different neighborhoods, he's moving from upstanding citizen to gutter trash. He knows that most of the fuckers like him get caught because we're already looking where they'll strike next, but they still do something stupid like pick up a whore right in front of us. I figure the only way we get this fuck knuckle in cuffs is if he gets cocky and fucks up."

"You, are a real fucking joy to work with, do you know that?"

"Two of my three ex-wives would testify to my being a joy in court. The other one has better taste than that."

"So, the Feds coming?" Hare changed the subject.

"Wait, you weren't polishing their knobs to make sure we keep our case? So why in the hell are you always late to these things?"

"I actually read case files in the office and follow shit leads, so I usually have further to go than you. If I did my detective work from a car seat parked outside a donut joint, I'd probably be here at the same time as you. And your faith in my heterosexuality is underwhelming," Hare replied.

"Hey, it wasn't an insult. Trust me, after three divorces and working on number four, I'll fuck anything that seems cool with it, I'm getting too old to be picky. But in answer to your question. Naw, they haven't been out yet. I bet they ambush you at the station and try and tie their cases in every city together into a big terrorist thing that they can wave around to the press when it comes time to ask for more funding," Burke said.

"And in the meantime, we have to do some real police work and try and catch the prick. You look like you're all snuggled up with your powdered grease so you can keep an eye on forensics. I'll go back to the station and try and figure out where we go from here. I mean, after I get to hear the Feds stupid ass theories about an international jihad against faces that is."

"Good enough, and don't talk shit about donuts like that."

They'd more or less broken the faceless one in the sub-basement now. He had a name before, but since then he had discovered that just like his face, he didn't need it anymore. The boy had acquiesced on his own to Bentley's use of him, offering himself just to feel anything; just as expected. While this was good, it would be better to have one of each though. While Bentley didn't view them as people, well the reality was one hole did feel different than the other. He was a man who liked variety.

Bentley was showering off the sweat of playtime in his mother's bathroom. He lathered methodically and carefully, rinsing as he went. Each spot was washed in a particular order, and no spots were missed that way. That was the way his mother had taught it to him, and that was the way he had taught it to.... to Ricky.

Ricky had such promise. He lit up every room just by walking in the door. His Dad had loved what he thought was his son, adored him probably more than he had Bentley at the same age, to be honest. Maybe Bentley couldn't be a real father to the boy, society wouldn't allow for that admission, but he felt confident going off to college that his son was in the best of all possible hands.

Bentley came home every break, just to see his son bound down the steps to greet him. The boy loved what he thought was his brother, and wanted to spend every moment together they could for the length of his break. Bentley brought girlfriends home as well. He'd honored his mother's wishes like a dutiful boy. None of them dazzled in his eyes the way she did, but they were all acceptable, interchangeable replacements for her.

Nothing good lasts forever.

He had just finished his finals when he was called into the Dean's office.

Somehow, his father had found out.

He'd shot and killed the three of them.

Bentley didn't remember much for a while. They told him that when they took him to the hospital he'd been hallucinating and raving. They did the only thing they could with him, drug him into insensibility. Until one morning, he lay there in the bed that he must have convinced the doctors he could be trusted alone in, and he had his mind back. Despite whatever medication they had him on creating a fog that he had to think through, it was clearer and more rational than it ever had been. Reality was finally opening its doors to him to reveal its full majesty.

He could see it all. The drones, the faceless ones, when they were confronted with blatant outright real humanity wouldn't be able to help themselves. They'd destroy it almost in self-defense. His drone of a father had. So, what now? Where did his father's actions leave Bentley? Well, for starters, with his family dead he was probably a relatively well-off young man. He had enough credits to graduate, even with any finals he might miss, so he certainly had a nice degree to go along with the money.

If he was smart and methodical he could do something about all the drones running around, couldn't he? The nightmare had proven to him what kind of damage a drone could do to real people. Bentley just needed to let care and caution be his by words. And he had, he'd slowly but surely been thinning the ranks of the easily replaceable. And it was better now than ever, after all this time he had a friend, a lover, a help mate, another human being to share the endeavor with. How broken he had been all those years ago. He had rebuilt himself, certainly, no one would be able to say he wasn't successful, the state of the house notwithstanding. But it wasn't until Patty came into his life that he realized that there had still been a part of him missing. A part that had died in a shotgun barrage so very long ago.

Ezra knew the hooker had thrown the cops for a loop. It was why he had done it in the first place. No, that wasn't entirely true, it took the edge off his needs, he had needed the slut every bit as much as she had needed to die. It bought him the time he could use to scout a house for a real bit of play. With the memory of the pleading whore fresh in his mind he didn't need to go flying in and make mistakes, he could be methodical about things. And he really was taking as much time as he could here and was joyous when that care and consideration paid off. He had the perfect little drone family all lined up. The important thing was to take his time and consider it, how he wanted to do it, the doing it without a trace, it was all vital to his success.

The Timmons family were each and every one of them drones. Dad who worked in upper middle management, stay-at-home Pilates mom, little girl in pre-school, and a little bun in the oven. There was not one single interesting thing about them. Their Facebook profiles looked identical to thousands of others just in the area. Completely replaceable flesh sacks.

It was only a matter of putting all his pieces in place, so he could take the pieces he wanted. He would make them matter; he would make them special.

John walked back to where the woman at reception had pointed. He weaved through cubicles carefully, he didn't want to brush up against anything or disturb anyone. Not in a place like this, lord only knew what it would do to him. Finally, he stood directly outside the cubicle he had been pointed to. He looked down at a mid-sized man with brunette hair starting to gray. The man was talking in an agitated voice with someone on the phone. John was doing everything in his power to wait and not listen. Unfortunately, this gave him unwanted snippets of some of the surrounding conversations. This was not good, this was a hive of bees some kid had thrown a rock into, getting his own thoughts to focus enough so he wouldn't sound crazy would be hard.

He heard the landline clack down hard and turned back to see the man staring at him, "Can I help you?" The man's tone was exasperated, that was not going to be a helpful attitude.

"They told me you were the one who was interested in missing persons in the neighborhood where my sister lived," John said quietly.

"Have you reported her missing?" the man asked him.

"Just now, up front. I hadn't heard from her, she wasn't answering her phone, so I checked her apartment, Landlord started bugging me for back rent, and said he hadn't seen her. So, I came here, and they told me to talk to you," John replied evenly.

The man let out a gusting sigh, "Look I'm sorry.... your name is?"

"John, John Rohrbach. My sister, her name is Carol."

"Look, John. I hate to be this blunt with a loved one, but I also hate to lie. Right now, this department is up to its eyeballs in a case. Like, all hands-on deck, especially mine. I'm sure you've seen the papers..."

"I'll be honest, I live out a ways from the city, don't watch a bunch of news. Seems most of it is just meant to get you pissing your pants about something that doesn't truly affect you one way or the other," John said carefully.

The man looked taken aback by that for a moment, then he smiled, "Smart man. Wish more people followed your example. Well, since you don't know, we have a serial killer on our hands. One that's started hitting the burbs a bit, and that's when the noise gets really loud around here."

"What if I found you your killer, would you have time for my sister then?" John said calmly.

The man laughed ruefully and then looked more carefully at John. Finally, he said, "I will tell you for honest and true, you help me nail the son of a bitch I'm after, and I will follow you through hell on a path of broken glass to find out what happened to your sister."

"You have a card?"

The man looked a bit shaken by the matter-of-fact calmness John kept replying with but found one in a little holder on his desk and passed it to John.

John read it carefully, "Well, Detective Bill Hare, hopefully, there won't be any glass along the way."

Bentley puzzled at it bemusedly. He had been his own man for years, he had picked his own victims, he had done his kills, and cleaned up after all on his own. Yet here he was letting Patty take the lead on the woman they'd be keeping as a pet. More and more he'd been letting her take the lead on who they chose. It shouldn't matter to him, they were all drones, they all deserved to die. Hell, that was the original arrangement that saved her life if he considered things honestly. Her ability to find the meat more safely than he could was what had stayed his hand. Watching her operate, he appreciated her all the more, he had come to depend on her deeply. Patty brought something else to the table, a sense of justice. She had a way of picking ones that maybe deserved it a little more, who not only would nobody miss, but quite a few would probably rejoice. Except for maybe that last girl, that had seemed like convenience to him. Which puzzled him, since her actions toward the girl had been especially vicious. There was some resentment there he didn't quite understand. If Bentley could resurrect the drone that had been his father, he would have been one of Patty's usual choices for the table. He would have been made to suffer dearly for the crime of killing his wife and Bentley's son. Bentley had always chosen based on ease of acquisition, but when Patty chose, he always felt like they deserved what they got. She had increased the morality of a holy mission even if that wouldn't have seemed possible before her.

Tonight, they were going to grab a meth head. According to Patty, she wasn't all torn up yet the way most of them were. But the reason she wasn't was why Patty wanted her. The woman would let her life spin out of control, Patty would have to come and rescue her poor son again and put him into foster care. A month after that, the drone would be in rehab crying about how she missed her baby so much and she was doing it all for him. A month after that, the kid would be back with his mother. Only to restart the same damned fucked up cycle all over again six months later.

The kid had grandparents who wanted him, who had taken him in the last time instead of forcing the kid into foster care. The Grandmother had cried when Patty had to drive the bitch there to pick the boy up. And after tonight, there'd be nothing in their way at all, the boy would just be theirs, and he'd finally be safe.

It was going to be simplicity according to Patty. The woman walked to her dealer's place completely unarmed. At night no less! In a perfect world, after she was safely tucked away back at the house, the new and more driven Bentley would take a couple of guns and walk into the dealer's place. But that would make a very public mess. There would be pleasure in lighting the place up, but right now all eyes were on their copycat, something like that would put them on the cop's radar like they'd never been before. Bentley, and now Patty, created disappearances, not bloodbaths that hit the front page of every paper. Hopefully, the dealer's own lifestyle would do the street cleaning soon enough. Or maybe one day they might have to find a way to get him all nicely tucked away in the Jeep to take a ride out of town.

Bentley was watching the approaching figure from the SUV. The woman was moving as quickly as she could along the dimly lit sidewalk heading back to her efficiency apartment. The way he figured, she might have gotten a taste at her dealer, but she was in a rush to get home and really load herself up. Bentley could just make out the woman's face when Patty stepped from the shadows.

The look on the woman's face was priceless, a little kid caught elbow-deep in the cookie jar. He could see her already beginning to try and play it off that this encounter was nothing important. Probably lying and saying she was coming from the store, without a damned thing in her hands that might have come from there. Patty had her hands on her hips, clearly saying she wasn't buying a word of it.

Showtime.

Bentley threw open the door of the SUV and got out, his gun already pointed at the pair of them. The woman's eyes were wide, Patty turned around slowly and made the same facial expression playing the role of innocent victim perfectly.

Before either of them could speak, Bentley growled loud enough for both of them to hear them, but nobody else, "In the fucking car, now, both of you. Or dead on the street, your call."

Their hands went up and they started inching their way toward the vehicle. Patty was keeping pace with the woman; the woman was obviously trying to buy time for a sudden rescue from a passerby or a chance to run for it. It most likely wouldn't happen. Bentley had chosen this spot on purpose, the streetlight was out here. Unless somebody turned down this street soon, nobody could see shit. For that matter, not many people down here cared even if they did see something. These people knew to mind their own business.

Still, no point in tempting fate, better to hurry it along. "Hurry the fuck up, you, the one that's dressed nice, there's some duct tape in the back seat, put the other one in the back and strap her hands and ankles. And I will be watching, so no bullshit!"

"Please Mister, we don't want any trouble," Patty said, putting a quaver into her voice like she was on the verge of tears. Bentley was proud of her, if he didn't know better, he'd totally believe she wasn't full of shit.

"Please, I got a kid," the woman pleaded.

"Well, the kid ain't here right now, and you won't be tomorrow if you don't get with the program right the fuck now," Bentley snarled and waved the gun to make his point.

The sobbing woman made her way to the vehicle, Patty's eyes gleamed as well, but that didn't stop her from winking at Bentley as she followed. Moments later tears of duct tape could be heard coming from inside the running vehicle. It went on for quite a while as it was spooled around the woman's feet and hands. Bentley had never learned the woman's name, and he was happy not to, it didn't matter to anything. Her name had never mattered at all, even less than the mask she wore.

Patty popped back out of the back seat and shut the door, "Trussed like Christmas ham. "

"All right let's get the fuck out of here before someone in this neighborhood develops a sense of curiosity," Bentley replied.

They had just exited the city when Patty couldn't hold it any longer. It started as a few snorts, then it became a chortle. Finally, she just slumped against the side of the door laughing. It took her a long time to finally get herself under control.

"What the hell got into you?" Bentley asked with a small smile he couldn't hold back as Patty's laughter infected him.

"Oh, I was just thinking. The drone back there is

finally going to get her addiction under real control, not just piss cup once-a-week under control. And despite that, the grandmother is still going to get her son," Patty panted out.

Bentley let out a bark of laughter, the conversation set off muffled screams from the back seat.

John had a laptop; he didn't use it for much normally. He only owned it because it helped him do the inventory and such for the farm at home. He was on Facebook, but he never used it beyond seeing if there were any updates from in town about any community events. The thirty friends he had on there were neighbors and friends from around the area. He talked to those people all the time, didn't seem much use talking to them when he couldn't see them face to face. Something about the cold, insensitive, impersonal nature of the internet bugged him. He was used to face-to-face conversations where if a man lied to you, you could tell he was doing it. On the internet people were whatever they could invent for themselves. It rubbed him wrong.

Tonight, he needed the infernal thing as he sat in Carol's apartment. He'd picked up the lease and paid the back rent, so in a way, it was his apartment now. It had taken a bit of talking, and some extra money after he'd approached the man to get the landlord to agree. Keeping the utilities on, including the internet he was using right now had been no small, or cheap feat either.

But it had been worth it just to have a base of operations that wasn't a hotel. He never really spent money back home except on the farm, so at least he could afford it. They were doing better than most farmers; their dad had snatched up enough land to not be bullied under by the bigger commercial farms or starved out by them. So instead, they were quietly ignored while they did a lovely farm-to-table business, including some of the better restaurants in this city. He'd rather be back there, overseeing work directly instead of by phone call, but it was what it was. The long and short of it meant that saving Carol's place in the world for her wasn't going to break him any, even if he knew she wouldn't be using it.

And here he sat in her existence instead of her, reading stories from various newspapers about the serial killings that had been happening here. While he knew Carol would never be found happy and whole, the stories gave him some solace, she hadn't died by this guy's hands. No, this one wanted people to see his handiwork after he'd finished, he displayed his victims as if they were his art. If Carol had been one of his victims, the body would have already been spread all over the front pages of these rags. The feeling he had gotten had been of great and lingering pain, but at least she hadn't been used as a prop so some sicko could show the world, he was so much smarter than they were. Even if the police didn't want to help with Carol, he wanted to help them now, he wanted the world to be rid of something so ugly and evil. It was his place in life to eradicate something like this.

He'd study, he'd memorize, he would learn the way this fucker thought. Hopefully, he could gain that insight, that sense, that something that would tell him more about the killer. He decided he needed a police scanner as well to see if he struck again. If John couldn't get into the monster's head by reading these articles and listening to these news reports, he could certainly do it at a fresh crime scene. John was just hoping to have this guy figured out before there was a next crime scene. He hadn't used his gifts like this since he'd gotten back from Iraq, he could only hope to get them back to that state where they'd be useful.

In Iraq, he had ignored his misgivings about the whole psychic thing and had just gone with it. He had wanted to live and come home, and they were his best bet to do it. The word psychic might make him uncomfortable, but less uncomfortable than dying on a roadside with your guts lying next to you. The thing with Carol back home didn't count as any great trick. John thought that he could see the guilt on the rapist's face even without his gifts screaming at him that this was the one who'd hurt Carol.

Tonight belonged to hope, hoping that Carol hadn't suffered long, and hoping he could put himself into the mind of a killer before he killed again. After that, he could let himself believe the hope that he could find who killed Carol with the detective's help. The world runs on people still believing in long shots.

"Be careful honey! We want to keep her remember?" Patty chided lightly. She reached down and grabbed the base of Bentley's cock and rubbed gently.

"It's just so... I never tried this before…"

"I know baby, but if you wedge that cock of yours into what little brain she has, we're going to have to get another one." She gently pushed Bentley back, forcing his cock out of the empty eye socket the bulbous head had been probing. She rubbed his gore-enshrouded member urgently, "Tell you what? Why don't you let Mamma finish you off, and then we can clean her up and sew her up? The other drone down there will be happy for the company once she stops screaming."

Bentley let out a groan when he heard her refer to herself that way. It was followed by another more forceful groan when she dropped to her knees and licked the blood and pre-cum from the head of his cock. As she began to bob her head up and down, a ring of blood formed around her lips as it sloshed off Bentley.

It wasn't until she was gulping hard to take his seed down her throat that they remembered the third party in the room. As the two of them had been moaning in ecstasy the woman who had so recently had her empty socket violated had been moaning in pain and confusion as to what happened to her. She had been abused sexually in her life, many times, if a dealer was going to cut you a break, he was most likely going to cut your skin. What had happened to her here was beyond any description she could form in her head, beyond any understanding of how the world worked.

They both chuckled to see they could forget themselves like that. Playtime was on hold, they went and washed their hands. Patty went and got some sanitized water, some alcohol, betadine, and some hydrogen peroxide from the rack behind her. Bentley unfolded a surgical wrap. As she cleaned the empty sockets he slowly and carefully selected a needle which he began to thread. His eyes squinted as he went through the process of feeding the surgical thread through.

He turned to the woman, whom Patty was just finishing with. He leaned in and with a gloved hand, pulled an eyelid out away from the socket, pulling it taut. "Well, I just want you to know, you're on the home stretch. I won't lie to you, getting stitches without anesthesia hurts like all fuck. But you've been through worse tonight, so keep the screaming to a minimum, huh? My hand might slip, and considering I have a very sharp fucking needle in it, right in front of your face, you probably don't want my hand slipping, now do you?"

All the battered figure on the table could manage was a soft moan, and then a whimper when he pierced the flesh of her eyelid and began pulling the string through.

Chapter 11

Where in the fuck was that dog? He better not have gotten out again. Johnathan sighed, odds were if he went out to the fence, he'd find her precious little rodent dog already digging around the fence trying to get out as per usual. Not that the little pea brain had a clue as to what he'd do if he ever actually obtained his freedom. It had cost Johnathan 200 bucks the last time the little bastard escaped. He had to put out a reward because otherwise Trish and Penelope would have thrown a complete shit about it. He'd better get the thing tonight, or there'd be another 200 bucks shelled out to some neighborhood brat with quick eyes and a piece of hot dog as bait.

Johnathan didn't bother with a flashlight. He had discovered long ago, as useless as a predator as the thing was, if he came up to it in the dark he could scoop it right up mid-dig. On the other hand, if he used the flashlight the little mongrel would treat it like some kind of game, and it would keep scampering just out of reach for half the damned night.

He could just make out its fur in the dim light over by the shed. Funny, it wasn't digging. Oh God, it could be worse, a rat could have died or something, it could be eating it and rolling in it! He rushed over and went to pick the little thing up. His hands touched moisture, still warm... What the hell?

Johnathan saw a flash of movement from behind the shed.

Ezra stared down at the little girl for a long time. He felt almost bad about the kids, he hadn't as much the first time, but he'd had time to think on it and now it bugged him. The father getting an axe in his fucking head, no issues with that at all. He'd read up on these people and if the dad had any personality at all it could best be described as "mayonnaise." He didn't even have interesting outdoor activities, the fucker golfed. The look on his face when he saw the axe coming down on his head had been fucking hilarious.

But the kid, who knew what she'd be with time? He considered, just like he had the last time, if he could just bind and gag the thing until this was over. A trauma like this would make for a pretty damned interesting adult, no doubt about it. A shake of the head, Ezra knew the answer was no. Kids have a habit of waking up and letting loose with the lungs. A kid could bring half the neighborhood into the picture if Ezra wasn't careful. He'd just have to suck it up, you didn't get to be a real person in life without occasionally doing something you didn't care for. Humanhood was being able to suck it up and do the hard work.

He thanked God he kept the big knife razor-sharp as he clamped his hand over the girl's mouth. Her eyes opened a little groggily as she tried to make sense of something that had no place in her world life experience. A moment later those same eyes opened up big and wide as the blade bit all the way down to the bone of her precious little throat.

A small sigh escaped Ezra as he saw the spreading stain working its way through her pristine white sheets and comforter. He really didn't enjoy killing the kids as much, but sometimes to save humanity you have to kill some bystanders. He reminded himself that trauma was no promise of later humanity. She could have just as easily ended up being a clone of her mom with massive therapy bills. Write it off to collateral damage that couldn't be avoided.

The hard part was over, now it was time for the main event.

Trish Timmons and her little upcoming bundle of joy were all he'd been able to think about for weeks now. And he was finally just a few short steps away from paydirt. The husband was fun, even the designer dog had even been enjoyable, but a preggers drone lying there waiting for him? Oh, it was to die for, or, to kill for more precisely.

As he opened the door, he heard a sleepy voice say, "Johnathan?"

Ezra was quickly over to the bed. He smiled down, "Not Johnathan sugar tits. But, if you don't want precious little Penelope to get involved in this, you'll do exactly what I say. Do you understand me?"

The whites of terrified eyes shone up at him in the gloom. But even in the dark, he could see the head nod. He took a roll of duct tape out of the bag he carried, "Good girl."

A tear of tape rent the air. A moment later there was another, and then another, and then another, and finally one last one. Trish's eyes watched him as if mesmerized the entire time. When he was done with the duct tape Ezra looked at his handiwork. She was perfection there in the moonlight, arms, and legs tied to the head and foot of the bed with both duct tape and zip ties. Her precious Johnathan's blood-stained tighty whiteys he'd brought with him from outside stuffed in her mouth, and a piece of duct tape holding it in place.

He smiled, best to be truthful, "It's just you and me babe, Johnathan and the pup are cooling out in the yard, and little Penelope has gone and made a bright red mess out of her bedding. I guess you could say she's a real woman now. A real dead one."

He waited for her muffled screams and thrashing to subside a bit before he continued. He ignored her while he undressed. "You know, seems to me, we got one too many guests at this party still." He held up a scalpel and let it catch the moonlight, so it glinted. "But you know, I watched a few videos on c-sections, and I think I can just about pull it off.... or out."

Ezra thanked all the gods on earth that the bitch was gagged. The way she was screaming as he made his incision would have told people the next block over what was happening to her. The first incision revealed the white of fat and protective layers, so he carefully made the second incision through the abdominal muscles and the uterus. Normally he knew that should be avoided, but it wasn't like he intended to sew her back up.

He pressed a bit, and let the amniotic fluid run over her belly and into the sheets. It should have been suctioned off, but again, he wasn't aiming for surgeon of the year here. Slipping his hand inside the wound he created, he had the head of the child in his hand. Ezra carefully cut more of the woman away to ease with removal, the flesh should be pulled away, but all he wanted was the damned thing out, not a healthy baby. Tugging slightly, he removed it from her body, his intent was to lay it in her arms while he improved her. As the feet came free, Ezra was shocked when the thing let out a choked little wail. He panicked, grasping the feet, he swung the infant viciously. There was a loud thump when it hit the nightstand. The crying stopped.

He carefully set the dead infant in its mother's armpit, turning the head so he didn't have to see the eyes that were dangling now that they'd popped out from the force of the blow. He took a deep sigh to compose himself. Now it was showtime. And best of all, she was still alive to enjoy some of it.

He held up his bloody scalpel, "Don't worry baby,

now that the distractions are out of the way, I'm going to give you the makeover you so deserve."

Later, Ezra decided that he was getting better and more efficient at this as he shoved her skin into the carry bag and gave it a shake to spread the salt evenly. He had been impatient all night, risking getting the dog, the husband, or the girl's blood on him. And he was still impatient, he might even be able to enjoy this fuck doll twice before he had to leave if he hurried. Tonight, had been efficient as hell, even with multiple extra bodies involved, with fast work comes longer pleasures.

He took a moment to appreciate the contrast between the red of her head and her pale white skin as he slipped on a condom and positioned himself on top of the cooling body. He was shocked, he didn't even need lube tonight. Some of the amniotic fluid and the blood had moistened the corpse's pussy to the point that it almost felt like the live act itself. Right then he was sure of it, he was going to have to fuck this one twice before getting out of there. It would be a good long while before he found another pregnant drone, best to get the most out of the moment.

John had been reading quietly in Carol's apartment when the scanner he picked up squalled to life. A 10-55, corpses, 104, murder. John snapped to and grabbed a pencil. He scrabbled the address down as dispatch gave it. With luck, he could get close enough to the scene that he'd be able to feel the killer. Let what he was wash over him, to give him the scent. It was never a name or a face, but a deep-down feeling. Once you felt the traces left by someone like that, committing an act like that, you'd never forget them. If you came anywhere near them, you'd know, you'd feel the glow of it on them even if you couldn't see them.

Carol never told John who'd interfered with her, but John knew anyway. Nothing gave away a man in Iraq who was about to open fire, but John knew anyway.

He locked the door and ran down the stairs to his truck.

"Fuck me gently with a chainsaw," Hare said when Burke had gotten out of his car.

"What? You getting here before me for a change?" Burke replied as he slammed his door.

"It's worse this time," Hare replied solemnly.

"How in the fuck could it get worse?"

Hare shook his head, "You want me to tell you first to prepare, or you want to go see for yourself?"

This caused Burke to pause, he hadn't given Hare that option at the previous house, but here his partner was giving Burke the choice. That sounded pretty bad. "All right, I am willing to go into this prepared, so I don't blow chunks at a crime scene, spill."

"Husband, wife, little girl, family dog, anddddddd....fuck, their unborn child. He cut it right out of her and bashed it," Hare said solemnly.

"Fuuuuuuuckkkkk."

"Yeah, and that ain't all. See the guy over there who looks like the stick is so far up his ass his tonsils are getting splinters?"

"How could I not, he looks like AI created Captain America."

"That is Federal Asshole, Andrew Bostic. The fedaralis are trying to figure if this is the work of copycats, or some fucked up network of terrorists, just as you predicted. Personally, I think the local office just wanted to look at gross dead bodies, but that's only my opinion," Hare explained.

"One I second," Burke seconded.

"So, we will be conducting our investigation today while trying to avoid someone from the Federal Bullshit Instigation, won't that be fun? Good thing you had me tell you, blowing chunks on a blood stain would have looked like shit."

"Yeah, they already think we can't find our ass with both hands and a map. How bad is it?"

"Well, worse than the last suburban setting, some stink from the woman from where he.... took the child out. I would say pretty fucking horrible all around... I've got no plans to sleep tonight."

"The boy scout checked it out yet?"

"Went in briefly then came out toot de damned fucking suite. I assume he'll let us gather all the evidence and then demand copies to look at. You done stalling?"

Burke nodded, "Yeah, I think that last coffee is just about digested, let's go get a look at my nightmares for the next couple of fucking weeks."

They were both standing by their cars later, not saying anything. What did you even say? They had no real evidence, they had brutalized meat and blood and not much else. Maybe forensics would get something this time, gods, they both hoped and prayed they would. But if they didn't, the two of them had just borne witness to the end result of a snuff film and they'd been put on janitor duty.

The guy just seemed too damned smart about it. No prints, no DNA, not even any fucking fibers as far as they could tell. Not a fucking thing on a single one of the victims. It was only a fucking miracle that the guy wasn't sending them, and the newspapers love letters about how he was killing with impunity, and telling everyone who would listen that there'd be more. Writing little manifestos that the papers would dutifully print in the name of "news" was par for the course for these psychos. The reality was, all those missives from the bastard, once they were in print, they'd be the inspiration for the next fucking nutter, just like that email had been. The only thing they had from the scene was that another neighbor had said something about a truck, just like last time, and just like last time the only description they could feel comfortable giving was "big and white, or maybe gray, or silver it was dark," which helped not at fucking all.

At least the Fed had not bothered with discussing much with them.

At least they were spared that small amount of ignominious humiliation.

Hare looked up to see a pickup truck turning around and parking just past the police barrier. He couldn't be a hundred percent sure, but he was almost positive that the guy driving it was the same one who'd come into his office about a missing sister or something.

"I'm gonna' head out, wanna' check a lead," Hare said flatly.

Burke's head snapped up, "You got a fucking lead, and you didn't tell me?"

"Did I say lead, I meant wild goose chase. But it beats sitting around here thinking about what we just saw. More of the psychic helps police variety of goose."

Burke snorted, "Normally I'd bust your chops, but you know what? Go hang out with Houdini if it gets us one step closer to finishing this thing. Bullshit mumbo jumbo is still better than anything we got on the scene."

Hare walked up to where Johnathan had parked his truck. The man rolled down the window as he saw the detective coming.

"Please tell me the reason you're here is that you're lost," Hare opened with.

The man looked blankly at him, and then realized he was being fucked with, "I need to feel him if I'm going to catch him for you."

"Uh-huh, I do not even know what that means. You know I'm not letting you any closer than this to an active investigation, right? I mean even if there wasn't a Fed over there, which there is?"

John nodded, "Yeah, that's fine. Somebody does something as ugly as this, you can feel them all the way out here."

"Look, I tried to say this before, but maybe I wasn't clear, I don't know if I can help you with your sister. I don't even have proof of a crime," Hare replied.

"You'll help, I know you will. When your dad, when he drank, didn't your mom always say you were her little helper," John replied, his big soulful eyes looking far away as if what he was seeing wasn't the where or when they were in now.

Hare looked stunned for a long moment. Finally, he said, "You mind if I talk to you about this in the truck?"

"Can you believe this shit?" Bentley growled.

Patty picked her head up from his chest to glance at his phone, which he was glaring at. "Which shit would that be?"

"The paper is describing our little copycat, pretty lurid details of course. The sheep need something to bleat at. Anyway, sounds like this weirdo is fucking them post-mortem," Bentley said.

"Good."

"Good, how in the hell could that be good? That's not how we do things," he looked at her perplexed.

"I agree it's gross and nasty. Do not get me wrong there. Still, good though. After this runs in the paper for a while, nobody on earth will give a flying fuck about something as petty as a simple missing person. Not for years after this. The guy is a gold mine, he couldn't be better if we hand-picked him for this," she smiled and then put her head back on Bentley's chest.

The female's training was coming along nicely. She seemed more pliable than the male had been at first. Not that the male had been that hard, but he'd offered them resistance. When your choices in life are cattle prod and fucking you tend to choose fucking relatively quickly, but he needed a couple of good shocks to lay out his choices for him. At this point, he'd probably roll over and beg if you told him. But the female, now that her lack of a nose was beginning to heal up, she wanted to please. They didn't ask her why; they didn't want to humanize her with conversation They just accepted her broken soul as a part of their personal toy and moved on. One day when Patty went downstairs and declared that her pussy needed to be eaten out, the female had volunteered like the smart kid in class. The drone had come to love her station in life. Who knew what detoxing in this environment would do to the human mind? But one thing it did do was make their lives easier.

Patty watched the two of them now silently from the stairs. She had snuck in here as carefully as possible not to disturb them. The door had been hell to get open quietly, but she'd managed. Their cages were next to one another but separated by bars. That didn't stop the two of them from playing around a bit. Bentley stood behind Patty and grinned, everything had worked perfectly, they had gone full bonobo, reacting to every one of the massive stressors in their life by frantically seeking the sole pleasure that he allowed them, sex. They had a TV, even if they had no access to the remote, of course, it was currently on the home shopping network, a few days ago it had been on MeTV. Nothing to give them information about the real world, nothing to upset them. They could also talk to one another, which was something Bentley had worried about.

Instead, they were fucking through the bars.

"Well, well, well, what do we have here?" Bentley called out loudly.

Neither of them could help but snicker at how the two drones lunged away from each other like teenagers caught by Dad. Even without most of the features that make a face, theirs both managed to convey the shame of being caught. Both of them managed to practically lunge as far away from the other as they could go. The male had ended up tumbling onto his butt where he sat in a frightened lump.

"It's all right," Bentley laughed. "Nice to see you like each other, being as you're neighbors and all. But what are we going to do with you now that we're down here?"

Patty leaned her arm over his shoulder, "Well, I suppose you could fuck her, I mean she is all warmed up and ready to go. I know she can eat some pussy, so that's me covered." She appeared contemplative for a moment before she said, "I suppose, since he's been such a good boy lately, I can suck a dick."

With their facial features reduced to lips and cheekbones, it would have been hard for most people to see it, but both of the drones were enthusiastic at the prospect.

"Yeah, I suppose we'll do just that," Bentley grinned. "Let me let the boy out and put his lead on him for walkies over to her pen."

They weren't particularly worried about mischief on the part of their charges. When the training began, they'd wired them both with shock collars. It would be stupid to use them in this situation, considering all four of them would be in a daisy chain, but neither the male nor the female had been a problem after a few times getting reminded of their place. They knew the cage was locked, and even if they could get the keys and manipulate them by touch alone, there was still a set of stairs and another locked door, and then even more things to negotiate past after that. And why would the drones even want to bother, their life was down here in the basement. There was no hustling here, no coming down here and scrambling to find your next high, no rent, no food to buy, just fucking and bad TV.

No, the drones were happy to have some excitement and pleasure in their lives, just like Bentley had predicted they'd be. The male didn't even complain when Patty put pressure with her teeth on his cock. What he didn't realize was that she'd had to remind herself that he was a permanent part of their collection, and she couldn't just bite it off.

There were plenty of other victims out there. It might be a cool way to kill one while Bentley ass fucked it.

John cruised slowly through another suburb, just not too slowly. He couldn't move too slowly or too quickly, people were on edge, they might call him in to the cops for being suspicious. Which would be ironic but would probably not help his relationship with the detective. He knew what he was looking for was out here somewhere, he was positive it wasn't a city dweller, that didn't feel right. To some people, this might feel like looking for a needle in a haystack, but not to John. John didn't have anything else to do. He had been doing this all day, every day and night for a week now. You hammered at your job as long as it took you to get it done. Plowing a big field started with climbing on the tractor.

He was just about to make the turn to drive back to Carol's when he felt something. He was almost prepared to let it go as just a distraction, the psychic equivalent of a flash of light from the corner of your eye, but he knew better. He turned his truck in the direction of the twinge and followed it. It became something else as he continued, something like a path laying out in front of him, a direct line painted through the world as he went. A dark path. He'd felt the presence of it at the murder house when he'd been there. He couldn't follow it then; he could only taste it, too much other info. The place was full of people, coming and going, many of them thinking vile thoughts about what they'd like to do to the perp, all that hatred spreading out like multiple tracks to a bloodhound. But not out here in the clear. Here, there was only one source, one direction, one path.

He had their man.

When the detective had barked at him about being on a crime scene, he'd let something slip. He knew it wasn't John behind this despite him showing up at the crime scene in a truck. While a truck had been mentioned as being unusual or out of place at both of the crime scenes where people gave statements, it hadn't been a red truck. It hadn't been John's truck. Instead, it had been either white or silver or gray, it was hard to say for certain at night, just not red.

A white truck with stickers in the back window. Just like the one sitting in the driveway of the house, John cruised slowly by. John smiled, guess it was time to find out if the detective had really meant they had a quid pro quo.

Bill Hare slowly drove by the house in an unmarked for a second time. The truck met the description they'd gotten on the two suburban murders, it certainly looked big enough to kill a hooker in the extended cab. The problem was a lot of people had these stupid big trucks out here. Guys that had never seen a construction site in their lives made sure they had something Ram Ford Chevy Tough in their driveway. How in the hell was he going to justify going in without a description of the guy himself?

He sure as shit was not going to be writing down in anything in any official reports that said his psychic buddy had pointed the perp's house out for him. God damn it, they had a truck matching the description, they had suspicion, even if it was weird as fuck. They had everything other than a reason to go in and try and stop the killing.

Fuck it, he needed to talk to Burke. His partner could be a pain in the ass, but sometimes he was a clever one.

Burke was already seated in the diner when Hare came in, his hair tousled from his hat, his head turned down in the direction of his food. How in the hell his co-worker had even found a diner in this day and age was beyond Hare. The fact that he had found one that still believed in price points and portions that had gone the way of the dinosaur during the Clinton administration was nothing short of impressive. As soon as Hare stepped through the glass and gleaming steel door a waitress started moving toward him to seat him. Hare made a point of pointing to where Burke was seated wiping out something of a heart-clogging nature and made his way in that direction.

"How in the hell do you find these places," Hare said as he sat down.

"Do I bitch about your uncanny ability to find a taco truck, even at midnight?"

"No, because you like tacos too. And who in the hell said I was bitching? I like diners, there just aren't many good ones left anymore."

Burke smiled, "And they know my name in every single one of them in this city. I put in your order, cheeseburger, and fries; I'm buying so don't bitch. You owe me tacos."

The waitress headed toward them, but before she even came close enough to talk, Hare just pointed at Burke's coffee and then himself and smiled. She smiled back and went to bring the carafe and a cup. Setting it down in front of Hare she asked, "So, you want to make any changes on what he ordered for you? Chef doesn't have it on the grill yet."

"Could you toss on some bacon?"

"Sure enough, darlin'" the middle-aged, plump waitress smiled and whirled back toward the counter. Hare watched her as she went. He'd never got married, always too busy, and for that matter too angry at the world he saw every day. He was currently single because of it, and he had to admit the forty-something waitress's hips had a certain swish as she walked that made him think about calling her his next ex tonight.

"Leave her alone, she's the love of my life," snarled Burke.

"So, when I tell that to Amy, she'll be thrilled. Finally, an excuse to be rid of you now that the kids are in college," Hare grinned.

"Enough bullshit banter, what are you going to do?"

"No fucking clue. Seriously. Guy fits the normal serial killer profile, the truck matches the description, he has a couple of priors for assault in his early twenties. Since then, he is 100% a model citizen. The guy is a fucking stereotype practically, and I'm afraid to move in because the main thing I got fingering the guy is a god damned psychic. Hell, our profile we had made doesn't match. Find me the judge that gives me a warrant with that bullshit," Hare spewed his exasperation out. That was the point of this little talk today, to try and figure out a way to move in with as little as they had to go on.

"I got an idea, but you ain't gonna' like it," Burke replied.

"Do you think it will work?"

"Might."

"Like it already."

Burke nodded, then said, "Fake tip to Bostic."

Hare shook his head, "He would never fall for it, the Feds are smarter than that. He'd be sitting on less than we have, and then he'd be duty-bound to call us in on it. He wouldn't risk the embarrassment."

"Ah, that's where I think you're wrong. I think he's just enough of an egotistical glory hound that he'll go poke his nose in, stop by, ask a few routine questions all on his own." Burke opined.

"He couldn't possibly be that fucking stupid," Hare countered.

"Well, if he is, you owe me a beer. Tacos taste delicious with a nice cold one."

Chapter 12

Ezra heard the motion sensor go off. He was down in the basement watching TV while Sasha was off doing some shopping. The house was empty, and nobody should be coming here today. Not now. He kept tight control of their social life, and today's docket was empty. He took the Springfield out of its shoulder holster in an instant. On his way to the stairs, he grabbed the Bushmaster from its resting place by the bottom step. Ezra was more than aware of his position in this life, he knew the new world order would come eventually. He was no fool, he knew he was forcing their hand by striking out at their drones. Sooner or later, they'd strike back, and knowing that meant there was no such thing as paranoia anymore.

The doorbell rang.

Instead of going toward the door, he went to his den on the first floor. Flicking a few switches told him everything he needed to know about his situation. There on the exterior cameras, standing on the custom brick porch, was a cop. It was absolutely a cop. The car in the background was a cop car, unmarked but unmistakable, he could even see the grill between the front and back seats on the camera that covered the road. The man standing there being filmed by his door cam was also absolutely a detective of some kind. Nobody just shows up at your house dressed like that, suit, tie, even a hat on a sunny day. Even the Jehovah's Witnesses dressed more casual these days, Ezra watched him for a second, he caught a glimpse of his belt holster when his dress jacket moved a bit as the man fidgeted.

Ezra smiled. It all came into focus now; the final scene of the passion play that had been his life. You don't write a manifesto if you expect to just be able to safely make a YouTube video and proclaim it to the world. You take those printed-out papers and put them in a hidden shrine to be dutifully reported after the fact. When you attack the status quo by yourself, you have to expect it to attack back at some point. And you have to expect them to bring crushing force when they do it. He had always known this was how it ended, he might not have admitted it to himself all of the time, but he knew in his heart of hearts.

The only question that remained was how he was going to go out.

He knew that too, and his smile grew wider. The cop was in for a surprise.

Bostic debated ringing the bell again so he could say he'd done due diligence and get the hell out of there. For all he knew this was just another dead end and he was just standing here looking like an idiot. Anonymous tips were ninety percent bullshit. He so didn't want it to be, if he could wrap this up solo, he'd be a god at the department. The envelope that had been delivered to him hadn't contained much. Just a pasted-together note, like old-time ransom notes, but that had been enough to want to check it. It had the name, the address, and a description of the truck. And one word at the top, Koh. The name the press had been using for the killer, it referenced some kiddie shit, face-stealing monster, or something.

Did he want to be scooping local yokels of their crime beats all his life, or did he want to get his own cases? Did he want to go somewhere in the agency, or spend the rest of his life getting sent out to shadow detectives to "establish a presence?"

He reached for the doorbell again.

The door swung open causing Bostic to jump back in surprise.

A man was standing there smiling. His smile didn't match his eyes which looked manic. He said evenly, "Hello drone."

His hand came up holding a gun.

He used it to shoot Bostic right in the throat.

Ezra looked down at the cop bleeding out on his doorstep. Well, no way they'd be able to miss this clue, huh? Oh well, in for a penny, in for a pound, Ezra dug his pocketknife out of the little sheath on his belt and flicked it open. Ezra straddled the drone who was bleeding out rapidly, his eyes looking around wildly, trying to figure out what had happened and why he was suddenly so weak. All thoughts of future glory had vanished, only to be replaced by white-hot pain, confusion, and ebbing strength.

Ezra set the blade of the knife on the bridge of the cop's nose. He tapped it there as if he was in thought.

"I ain't done with you quite yet," he smiled.

He then dug the blade into the man's right eye socket. A gurgle of protest came from the dying drone beneath him. The eyeball popped instead of coming out all the way. That was OK, at least for what came next.

Ezra unzipped his pants.

It was all about how you wanted to go out he thought as he inserted his rock-hard cock into the dying cop's eye socket. He was going to thumb his nose at the drone army and the drone system one last time by skull fucking one of their enforcers right on his front fucking lawn. They were coming to kill him, but they'd never be able to gun down this image. Let the neighbors see it all, that way they'd know what was coming for all of them soon enough. There were enough humans out there, and at a kill ratio of twelve to one like he'd managed since he'd seen the light, each and every one of their skulls was going to get dick probed before this was all over. Let them all see that the authority of the drones that they all worshiped could be vanquished by the blood slimy rock-hard cock of a real man.

Ezra could hear the sirens approaching as he started to feel his orgasm building up.

"Jesus Christ! Get away from that man with your hands up!"

Ezra brought his gun around to fire at the cops.

The neighborhood erupted with the sound of God knocking down the walls of Jericho.

During the search of the house, the building had yielded its secrets to the officers relatively easily. What Ezra had been able to hide from his wife was no match for a crowd of anxious detectives. Burke and Hare were standing in a small room looking at a row of tanned leathery faces. Both were silent for a long time. As horrific as the crimes had been, the trophies made it worse somehow. Normal serial killers just took jewelry for the love of fuck. They could see the stack of paper waiting for them as well, clearly labeled, "The Rise of the Humans," which they both knew was going to be a lengthy manifesto, and that they were both going to have to read the thing.

Finally, Burke broke the silence, "This, might be one of the most fucked up things I've ever seen."

"Weirder than watching somebody skull fuck a federal agent on their front lawn?"

"I showed up late, they'd already shot the fuck out of him by the time I pulled up," Burke shrugged.

"Lucky bastard. I have no idea how in the hell I'm going to write that up. 'Semen found in victim's orbital socket,' just doesn't seem to cover it. I pity the coroner on this one."

"So, what's next on your agenda?" Burke asked.

"You mean after the ton of paperwork this is going to take? Avoid the press like the plague, try to fend off book deals, and go help that psychic guy with his sister," Hare stated.

"You're actually going through with that?" Burke was incredulous at the thought.

Hare stared at his friend, "How many more bodies do you think we're looking at if he doesn't tip us off to old Ezra here? I owe him."

They were silent again, their eyes roaming over the horror laid out in front of them.

It was Burke who broke the silence again, "Can you believe this fruit was fucking married? Kids in college no less."

"It fits the pattern with some of them. Green River was married. Herb Baumeister was married with three kids and sixteen bodies buried in the backyard. Wives didn't have a fucking clue."

"Ain't that some fucked up shit?" Burke replied.

"Turned out our shrink profile was a little off," Hare said.

"Fucking shrinks, what do they know?" Burke snorted.

The female screams were so powerful they could hear them all the way in the basement.

"Sounds like the Missus just got home," said Burke.

Sasha was staying in a motel room. She couldn't stay in the house, not after what she'd learned about Ezra. She almost felt like she couldn't even sell the thing in good conscience, best bet would be to burn it to the ground and salt the earth. Maybe when the police released Ezra's body, she could crucify him to the front door before she lit the match.

She had sat in her car for a long time, making tearful phone calls to the kids and to her sister. Explaining that everything she had thought her life was had been a complete fabrication. That the man she had wed twenty years ago when she was only seventeen, the man whose children she had borne happily, that man was a monster out of some dreadful movie she personally wouldn't have had the nerve to watch.

Her sister had practically pleaded with Sasha to stay with her. She couldn't, not yet. She wouldn't be able to tolerate the pitying looks, the secret thought behind those eyes of, "She slept with a monster and was too clueless to know it." For all the well-meaning nature of the offer, she just couldn't stand it. Everyone now knew that Sasha had been a fool, a fool, and an enabler to the worst beast humanity had to offer.

It was already getting dark when it dawned on her that she certainly didn't want to sleep in the car. So, she rented a room in the cheapest motel she could find. It didn't matter where, as long as she knew she wouldn't accidentally see a neighbor. All she was going to use it for was the walls inside for something to stare at, and hopefully to eventually fall asleep on the bed. She needed a place to figure out who she was, and who she was going to be for the rest of her life. It had been a question that she'd thought well settled for decades now. It turned out that hadn't been true at all, not even the past was settled anymore. The future in this situation was beyond her knowledge. She needed the time to figure out who the person was that was going to face it.

Sasha had forced herself to get some food, and with that food maybe a few drinks. Only a few. She didn't need to make a total ass of herself in public, she'd done enough of that already. Anyway, there were plenty more drinks waiting for her in the motel refrigerator. She had made sure of that first and foremost after checking in. Sobriety? She'd spent most of her life as sober as a church mouse, and what had it gotten her? Maybe real magic would happen for her tonight, which would be if she never woke up as she choked on her own vomit. It was roughly around ten as she walked back to the hotel. She was smart enough to know she was in no condition to drive. It was a miracle she had been able to drive to the motel before drinks considering how badly her hands were shaking.

Everything about life at this point was going

through the motions for her, just like it had been for Ezra every time she'd kissed him. She had gotten food because she realized that she hadn't eaten since breakfast and bodies needed food to function. She had gotten booze because.... well, that was what young widows did, they got hammered. If Ezra had let her have more friends outside the neighborhood, maybe she'd be at some best girlfriend's place sobbing away. Or maybe not, it was hard to beg for sympathy when you'd been sharing a bed with the vile thing, she had been for decades now. Even if you didn't know, you should have known that was the judgment of the world against this 37-year-old widow. God, there would be documentaries about Ezra, and there she'd be, the smiling clueless dipshit cooking his dinner every night.

She was in such a daze she barely registered the SUV that pulled up alongside her and was pacing her. It only got past the fog of her miserable thoughts when a female voice called out from the back seat, "Hey pretty lady, you look sad. What's wrong honey?"

Sasha froze in her steps, the mere concept that someone would be worried about her at all in all that had happened seemed so alien, her brain just locked up. Finally, she managed to mutter, "You have no idea."

"Want some company, we got a place. I hate seeing someone looking like you do right now," the female voice replied.

"I don't know if I could handle...."

"Naw, nothing like that, we're bored, on our way home, and....well, you just looked like you could use a friend. And just somebody new to talk to livens up our evening."

Sasha knew she shouldn't, every instinct her body possessed told her to run like hell and not stop. But then she considered every instinct her body possessed had told her that Ezra was the safe choice. He'd be a good provider, a good father.

The last she had seen of that good provider he'd been covered in a white sheet, and from what she'd been told his dick was still in an FBI agent's eye socket. Maybe her instincts would have to get a few right before she listened to them again.

She smiled weakly, "Sure, why not."

Bentley was a bit worried about this one. She was going along with things too easily. They hadn't had to drug her to get her to come into the house. Hell, even when Patty suggested they go down to the basement she'd come willingly. They'd finally drugged her drink on the couch down there to be sure there'd be no problems. But with the way she'd been acting, Bentley had been almost sure she'd traipsed in and strapped herself to the table.

They'd only roofied her, so she was still able to talk, so she'd still have some life in her while they liberated her. It was an experiment Patty had wanted to try. But even with the ability intact, the woman hadn't said much as they'd led her through the door into the chambers beyond the basement. She'd just whispered to herself, "Hey, score one for my instincts," when they strapped her onto the table and started cutting her clothes off. Worse, she had this little half-smile on her face the entire time, like what was about to happen was the punchline of a joke no one else knew.

She didn't even cry out when Patty removed her eyes, she just sighed, "Nothing I want to see anyway."

Bentley was getting so frustrated he was about to strike her when Patty pulled him aside into the tool room, the woman called after them, "Don't keep me waiting my darlings."

"What the fuck is up with her?" snarled Bentley barely able to control himself.

"I think she's in shock about something. I mean more than what the drug did, I was noticing it in the car. Something horrible must have just happened to her, I've seen it before," she explained.

"So, what in the fuck do we do with her?"

Patty laughed a little, "Come on baby, don't be like that. She's still a drone. I have no idea what that woman was doing in that neighborhood, but her clothing says suburban mom. We do to her what we do to all of them. You give her the best fuck of her life, and I'll make her look like what she is inside. Anyway, you deserve a better class of drone, there's no tatts, no scars, just pure

American faceless masses. I'd be willing to bet this one's even complained about the books in her kid's library and has a nice little soccer practice SUV."

Patty began to rifle through the woman's purse, as Bentley stood there considering it. She let out a whistle, "Oh, did I call that one right? Will you look at this address? Houses there go for three-quarters of a mil' on the low side. Bet you somebody had a fight with the hubby and is showing him a thing or two out slumming to have an adventure with nobody knowing where she is."

Patty looked at him and smiled, her eyes smoldered with a lust that was only partially sexual, "So while she's showing hubby a thing or two, why don't we show her everything she needs for the rest of her life?"

Bentley smiled, and cupped Patty's breasts eliciting a gasp, "Yeah, why don't we do that?"

Patty could see Bentley needed help the rest of the way. She almost became a presenter on a game show, giving him sultry looks as she presented him with an ear. Then another ear, and finally the nose itself. Bentley was more looking at Patty than what he was doing, the woman barely let out a whimper as Patty cut her to ribbons and Bentley fucked her.

At last, he could feel himself getting close to coming. Patty put the knife against the woman's throat. The woman weakly said to the heavens as the knife pressed forward, "Thank God it's over."

Bentley came, Patty slammed her mouth over the gurgling throat as hot red dripped around her lips while she pulled the dying woman's last breaths from her.

"Jesus fucking Christ will this case not fucking end?" Burke snarled.

"What now?" Hare sighed as he looked up from his desk.

"Glad you fucking asked. We went from a rotting Federal Agent with serial killer cum in his brain to now our lunatic's wife is missing?"

"What?"

"No shit, she checked herself into a motel. No surprise there, the house is a crime scene, and really, she might be estranged from her relatives and old friends. Guys like that tend to be controlling as fuck. Thing is, motel tells her pay for another day or vamoose, she ain't there. Her shit's there, bags, clothes, toiletries what have you, but no her. They wouldn't have even called it in, were just going to toss her stuff when I ran her credit card to track her down and called over there to speak to her," Burke said.

Hare just stared out into space, before he finally said, "So, you been over there?"

"Yep, and I got fuck all to go on. No sign of a struggle, fridge was stocked with hard seltzers, it honest to Christ looks like she just stepped out for a minute and never got back."

"Great, we close a serial killer, and we open another missing person. That's just swell. Speaking of which, in about ten minutes our little helper is going to be in here asking for help with his missing sister," Hare replied.

"What are you going to tell him?"

"I mean, I promised him I'd help. But I have no idea how helpful I can be. We got a bunch of missing persons around that area; we also don't have a single clue on any of them. I don't know, maybe the killer's wife will give me a way to make that point. People go missing a lot, but if we don't have a witness or some evidence, they usually stay missing for good."

Burke looked up, "You better put your notes away quick, it looks like your 2 o'clock just walked in the door."

"All right, I'm heading back to my cubicle, if anything shakes on the Bride of Leatherface let me know, don't be afraid to interrupt."

Hare looked at John and could see the anticipation on the man's face. The guy had every right to feel that way, and Hare's resentment of the situation was all on him as his problem, not John's. The detective might know it, but it didn't stop the feeling of irritation. Even if the guy asking the impossible of him had given him the lead that ended the reign of terror of a headline-grabbing serial killer. Even with that mitigating circumstance, the guy was still asking the impossible.

Hare sighed, "I don't know what to say, but have a seat anyway, let's figure it out."

John looked a little stricken but did as he was told. "Look, I know you don't have to do this. No one is going to believe you that I gave you some psychic tip-off. Hell, I don't want anyone to know I did, people think you're a weirdo if you claim stuff like that. I just want to figure out what happened to Carol and go back to my farm, probably to mourn her."

"I gave you my word John. I may get a bit grubby from what I have to investigate, and what I have to do to bring the bad guys in, but if a man's word is no good to someone who does him a favor...." Hare left the words hanging.

"Then he's as bad as his word is," John finished for him.

"I can give you a little bit of background at least. Maybe you'll have some insight that's just eluding me, hell, stranger things have happened. Those kinds of neighborhoods, there's always going to be a high rate of missing persons, it just comes with the territory. Nobody wants to live in a place like that, no shock if they leave. Worse, there's not a lot of incentive on the department's part to dig too deep. Before you say corruption, it's not that really. Quite a few get killed and some vanish, but even more, they have no real ties to the area, they just leave. Everyone likes to think Heaven is a place just in the next city over, all they have to do is get there. But I did notice an uptick, heck, that's been my busy work before old Ezra made life far too interesting for all of us, but really.... I just don't have any evidence to follow." Hare explained patiently.

"By no evidence you mean, what?"

"Hell, I don't even have anything, only the normal amount of bodies turning up at the morgue. I have no bodies, no witnesses, no nothing at all. All I have is an abnormal amount of missing person reports and familiar faces vanishing from our arrest roll with no proof of anything. I can't even prove there wasn't some mass exodus somewhere and nobody thought to mention it," Hare said dejectedly.

"Do you think they're connected in any way?" John asked, probing for the detective to give himself something, some sliver of hope to hang his hat on.

"Do I think so following the evidence? What evidence? Do I think so emotionally, it seems too much to be a coincidence. And the disappearances shift. Like, when there's just enough in one hooker hangout or one bad neighborhood, suddenly it moves to the next one before anyone can get a fix on it. Can I ask you something, and don't get mad? Do you think your sister ever hooked, or did drugs, something to get herself into a bad position? Be honest, it's the only way I can get a handle on things to hopefully find a starting point."

John was quiet for a long moment, finally, he said, "I don't think she did. She sounded the same when we talked, and I figure she would have sounded different to me. I'm not saying she wouldn't have, she felt ruined when she left home, whatever she was saving had already been taken, and she would have done anything to not come back after that."

"Again, I need truth and facts, did you have anything to do with that?"

John actually smiled wanly, "Only to make sure it didn't happen again."

Hare sighed, "So, she might have been hooking, if she had been she'd have just started. I'll come over to the apartment and give it a solid going-over so we're at least trying here. A lot of girls think they can just do it here or there from their place, maybe something got left behind."

"I think I would have noticed."

Hare was silent for a moment, finally, he said, "Yeah, I suppose you would have. Still, it won't hurt to look. Another set of eyes and all."

"True."

"Drugs?"

"She barely drank."

Hare tapped a pen on his desk in thought, "Now that does kind of make it interesting. Almost every missing person I've got had either drugs or prostitution or both in their background. Assuming it's another killer other than Ezra, the vics were someone the killer assumed wouldn't be missed. And they're right about that. In all the directions we get pulled by politics and other bullshit, anybody who doesn't look squeaky and sweet and wonderful on a missing persons or in a description to a jury can just about go fuck themselves. I don't like it, but it's the way it is. That was why I started digging at this jump in missing persons in the first place. It didn't seem fair to me that it just got ignored."

"But how does all that fit with Carol?" John interrupted.

"That's just the thing, it shouldn't, but I'm almost sure it does. Let me ask you another question, you think any of the girls in that building she lived in were working girls, as it were?" Hare asked.

John blushed a little, which looked strange on the big man, "I wouldn't want to speculate."

"I want you to, please, speculate away."

"Yeah, I think a few of them might," John admitted.

Hare nodded, "Now that's a start. They might have been working on her to join the ranks. Selling it to her as easy money. If she was getting strapped for cash, she might have been considering it. At least that gives us a starting point, ask around the building, see if anybody hooked her up with a john, and if so, what the guy looked like. We can start there."

"I've talked to a few, maybe I can see if they know anything," John offered.

"All right, you do that. Something fucked up has happened here at the station, it's going to keep me occupied for a day or two, but then I'll come by the apartment, and we can compare notes."

John left the station with less than he hoped for, but frankly, more than he expected.

Chapter 13

Bentley was at the cabin but not for rest or relaxation. He was packing methodically. He had gone to the cabin before without Patty, there was nothing suspicious in that. Frankly, there was nothing particularly suspicious in his packing now either. He had seen the papers earlier and what had been splayed across them like a lurid accusation to the entire world. Not only was their copycat deader than a door nail, a victim of a spectacular suicide by cop, but Bentley was pretty sure the man's wife was now so many cold cuts in his freezer at the moment.

He appreciated the irony of it, but it worried him. Some instinct said that it was time to take a lengthy vacation. He intended to bring Patty along, Bentley couldn't fathom life without her, but he wanted to have things wrapped up here before he told her. Then they could grab what they needed from the main house and her apartment and go without the opportunity for hesitation on her part. Animal intelligence told him that this looked like the kind of thing that created very bad heat and there were plenty of places to go for a while and wouldn't it be a lovely idea to visit them?

He didn't want to be distracted by her presence and therefore slowed down any in getting ready to leave if they had to. She was very good at being distracting, and he had a busy day planned. So, he made a judgment call to tell her when he was ready to ensure less of an argument. Not only did he intend to pack, but he also intended to do the kind of business transactions that ensured that even if this turned into a much more extended vacation than he wished, they'd be well stocked with cash. In his upbringing one thing that had always been stressed was that if you were well stocked with cash, life presented very few obstacles you couldn't overcome.

Patty had the house to herself while he wrapped up the cabin and got it ready for dry dock for a while. He'd said he had some maintenance to do up here, and she could use the house for whatever her heart desired until he got back. He couldn't help but wonder what she was up to today, all he'd told her was that he'd be up here for the night. No worry, he could check in later, after he was sure his finances were squared away and that his spare toothbrush was in his bag. This could still all turn out to be paranoia on his part, but one of the keys to life was being prepared. Ask any Boy Scout. And just because you're paranoid doesn't mean they aren't out to get you.

John had a new plan of action; he was lingering in the halls of the apartment building. Not in an obvious way, just going in and out a lot, taking separate trips for anything he needed instead of ganging them together. Taking his time, he moved down the halls and up and down the steps of the rotting building. Talking to the women who had introduced themselves when they'd seen him in Carol's apartment, burying his desire to be nosy about their lives with tepid small talk that he always led back to Carol. Trying to fill the blanks in on Carol's life in the city, hoping just one of those blanks was the one that led to what had happened to her.

The girls were nice to him, and he was pleasant back. They could tell he was hurting, and one of the things people learned down here at the bottom was that kindness was free, but it was also priceless. It was funny what you'd change your mind a bit about. These weren't the harlots from Sunday School here, inherently wicked and evil by their very nature. They were just women who were trying to put food on the table and a roof over their heads the only way they knew how. At least that's how he was beginning to see it. Yes, they took drugs, but what of it? Life had been hard, and most of the world these days was on one thing or another to get by anyway. Not everyone could afford to pill-shop doctors, there were other doctors out there who charged on a sliding scale, ones without degrees.

He was just heading up the metal stairs back to the apartment when he paused. He felt something, he felt something hard. A woman who was frankly too well put together to live here was leading another woman down the steps toward him. He moved out of the way and stared at them in shock that he forgot to hide.

The well-put-together woman smiled at him and

said, "I've never seen you in here before."

He forced himself to get some control of his emotions, "I'm Carol's brother, I'm looking over her apartment."

A look passed over the woman's face, so quickly you might not have noticed if you weren't looking as hard as John was. She quickly said, "Well, I keep an eye on quite a few of the girls in the building, I'm a social worker. My name's Patty."

She held out her hand and John shook it. A shock went right through his system. It was so strong he couldn't process it immediately; it was all he could do to not let it show on his face. He forced a smile and just replied, "John."

"Funny name if you're in this building. Well, I'll see you around...John." To the young woman trailing her she said, "Well, come along Sandra, the gentleman won't be impressed if you're late for your interview."

John watched them go down the steps for a moment before he rushed up to the apartment. If he hurried, he could follow them easily, just on the cloud of darkness emanating from that woman. But he damned well wanted his gun with him before he went. His hands fumbled with his keys opening the door. When he yanked the door open, he barely went inside, only quickly strapping on his shoulder holster and tossing his jacket on over it.

It was all he could do to not run down the steps

chasing after them. No sense in risking personal injury and drawing attention to himself as he went, he couldn't afford to get this wrong. He flew out the front door letting the hydraulics slowly pull it back into place behind him before heading for his truck. He assumed he'd be following her aura the whole way; it would be safer. John's head was dragged down the street by that feeling just in time to watch the woman seat herself in a sedan and close the door behind her.

Jumping into his truck, John forced himself to calm down and breathe. He could feel her when he was in his truck. If he could feel her, he could follow her. He knew it when she'd touched him, she'd had something to do with Carol's vanishing. A bad something. A bad something in a life that was replete with bad somethings, as bad if not worse than he'd felt from the serial killer Ezra. And something else, some sadness or longing lurking under it, something he couldn't get a handle on with the waves of dark nauseating hints of memories slamming into him in that instant. Ezra had all been hatred, sharp, and angry, this had some somber melancholic undertones and something else besides. Something that almost even felt like love.

The woman might not be all of the story to Carol's end, but she was enough of it. He'd track her down, get her alone, and then he'd know the rest of it from her one way or the other. John contemplated calling the detective but dismissed it. The detective would step in, arrest the woman, maybe, though on what evidence John was damned if he knew. Within an hour she'd be set free with an apology from the police. What the detective wouldn't do was let John get more of the story, to find out exactly how Carol fit into all of it. If he called the detective whatever happened after that would be the end of this road, and John couldn't allow that to happen yet.

He owed it to Carol to get it right. He'd gotten everything else so wrong from the moment she'd walked in the door that night. Everything his soul had told him was the right thing to do hadn't been, if it had been Carol would still be at home. John had taken one look at her when she fell in the door that night and had known what had happened. He didn't say a word to her, he hadn't known the words to say. He knew how the whole world felt about everything, damn it, but not a single damned word to make anyone feel better about anything.

Instead of giving her the hugs and platitudes she wanted, he had just gotten up, put on his jacket, and headed out the door.

Took him less than an hour to find the SOB. What happened after that took at least two hours, one to ensure he'd never do it again, and another to make sure the police never wanted to talk to John about it.

It was late when he walked into the kitchen of their

farmhouse. He had seen the bathroom light on when he'd pulled up in his truck, so he knew she was still up. John might have had no talent for it, no ability to say the right words, but he needed to make sure she was as all right as possible in the circumstances. It was his last duty of the evening. He walked slowly up the stairs, sighing a little, he didn't want to do this, he had already done the part he was good for. That didn't matter, the world demanded more of him, Carol deserved more of him.

John stood there in the hall wondering what to do when the door opened, and Carol stepped out with a towel wrapped around her. He could see bruising on her face, he could see the puffiness of where she'd been crying. She was his sweet, precious, sister, and she'd been hurt so thoughtlessly by someone.

He opened his arms begrudgingly.

She flooded into them and began to shake as she sobbed. He tried to pet at her hair, tried to whisper soothingly, "It's all right now's to her. None of it seemed sufficient to the hurt she received. She felt her head turn back, looked down, and saw her shining eyes staring up at him.

"My hero," she smiled, and then she kissed him. Not like she should have.

He wanted to break away, he should have broken away. This was taboo, this was sick, he distantly heard her towel drop to the floor. But he could feel her hurt, her need to be loved tenderly, the hope that it would somehow make all the violence that had happened tonight go away. John wanted to pull away, to tell her they couldn't, but John never had the ability to deny her. Especially when he felt that he was protecting her the way she felt he was now. If he told her no, she would know the vision she had of herself, as broken and disgusting, as trash, that it was all true, every word her attacker had called her. He couldn't allow that. She wanted the only man on earth she trusted to tell her she was still precious in a way that counteracted the violence she had just received.

When he woke up, he was alone in his bed. Getting up he went to the door and stepped out of his room into the hall, it was to see her packing through her open door.

"Carol, I am so sorry...." he began

She smiled sadly at him as she paused in her packing. "No, John. There's nothing for you to be sorry about. You avenged me, you comforted me, you did everything I'd want a man to do."

He went to speak, but she interrupted him, "Hold on, we both know what we did was wrong last night, but we both know it didn't feel that way, did it? And that's the reality of it John. Something I had been thinking about before last night, last night just set it in stone. I'll spend the rest of my life loving only my brother, allowing him to love no one but me, or I can leave. Because trust me, especially after last night, there isn't a damned single man in this county I want to waste my life with. Not one of them holds a patch on you."

She walked over to him and put her hand gently on the side of his face, "John, if we want a normal life, I have to go find mine."

He hadn't been able to talk her out of it, even more, she'd talked him into it. He found himself wishing her well, hoping that she could find some kind of life with someone less weird, less haunted than himself. He even tried to date some after she'd gone, but it was difficult. When you can feel what lurks under the surface of every person you meet, it took a special girl to clear that bar, and he hadn't found her yet. Mostly what he found were girls who had decided they were ready to settle down, and most importantly, wanted to do it with an eligible bachelor whose farm was doing that well. It was class fucking for the Farmer's Only set and he wanted nothing to do with it.

He came back to himself, to the here, to the now. Realizing deep down that while he might avenge her again, she had gone somewhere where there would be no comfort he could give her. Tears worked their way down the sides of his face, though his teeth were clenched his voice refused to whimper or whine. The woman driving that car knew Carol's fate. And he could feel that woman's trail flowing behind her with every mile that the truck rode over. He could afford to give voice to his pain when this was over, not before.

John made it a point to fall back, to be well out of the line of sight. There was no point in being right up on the other car, he could practically smell the trail of stench behind it better than any bloodhound that had ever been born. No, if his prey had the slightest idea he was back there, she'd run rabbit, head for a dense population, create a fuss, and become gone in the tumult that a few well-placed feminine screams could create. She'd be alert, she'd vanish, he'd never know.

He wasn't surprised when they left the city proper. What he felt coming from the woman would be hard to hide in a city, not impossible, just hard. Dahmer had proven how incurious people could be, but then again, Dahmer had been caught eventually. Easier to hunt in the city and feast somewhere else. He checked his gas gauge, thankfully it was doing good, because at this point even the suburbs were dropping away, and fields were starting to appear here or there. This close to what he wanted to know he wouldn't be able to bear pulling over and pumping the truck full. He'd walk first just to keep moving forward.

John smiled a bit when they turned onto what almost seemed like a country road. Yes, this kind of place would be perfect for what that woman did. It would be just as perfect for him today. He let his eyes dart everywhere to scan the surroundings, taking in the dark greens created by the sun, trying to force its way to the tree-lined road. He certainly wouldn't be pulling right up to the house; he needed a place to pull over once she reached her destination.

There, she'd pulled into a driveway. John didn't brake but drove by the house slowly just like normal traffic on a road like this. It would have been hard not to drive by slowly anyway, the road was really only a lane and a half. His target and the woman from the apartment building were both getting out of the car and walking toward the front door of a house. From what he could see before he'd passed and it vanished, down the drive was a relatively expensive-looking two-story, with a large piece of property surrounding it. Perfect for a murderer. He could only hope it would be perfect for him too.

John pulled over at a widened spot on the side of the road a bit past the house. He'd have to go on foot now which meant leaving the truck for a while. At least where he was parked looked like it had cars there parked on a semi-regular basis. Maybe there was good hunting, or maybe a trout stream nearby. He was hunting something far beyond any little bunny or placid fawn. John checked his gun and entered the woods.

John moved easily through the woods, he was a country boy, and he was in his element. Growing up, roads had only been suggestions; it had always been quicker and more fun to go in a straight line through fields and woods. You never knew what life would give you if you made your own paths.

Just by the way the light filtered through the trees he knew which direction would lead to the house. In this case, he didn't need his instincts nearly so much as back home. He could feel the woman. She didn't know it, but whatever she was doing right now, what she was really doing was waiting for him.

The edge of the woods came into view, and it was leap of faith time. He had to cross the overgrown grass to get to the place, it would leave him out in the open. John had to hope they weren't upstairs or didn't come out while he made a dash for it. Since he was on the garage side, it was the only way they'd spot him.

He ran.

Moments later he tried not to feel like a moron as he slumped against the side of the building. He was in decent shape, but it was farmer shape, and frankly, that didn't involve a lot of this commando running around shit. Iraq had, but that had been a long time ago. John was just starting to get his breathing under control when he felt it. Someone inside this house was in a level of pain he could feel right through the walls.

Not sparing time to think, he ran for the rear door of the garage. It swung open easily in his grasp. People in the country always forget that door for some reason. And thankfully, just like people always did, they had forgotten to lock the kitchen door that led out here as well.

John stood there in the kitchen trying to get a handle on so many things. First, he wanted to find where the pain was coming from, that seemed urgent. But the house itself confused his senses. It looked a mess, but that felt false, like it was a manufactured appearance that didn't really reflect the personality of the owner. But the house oozed with that personality, its walls were tainted with it, and it wasn't the woman. She spent time here, loads of it, but it wasn't her home. And the one who did live here was if anything just as dark and as evil as she was and every bit as wounded. No matter what happened here he may only be half finished with his mission when the sun dropped over the horizon to end the day.

But speaking of that mission, the pain. The pain that he believed was below him now.

He tried to keep his movements stealthy as he searched for the door to the basement. If the woman had the ability to cause such pain, there was no good reason to forewarn her. It took him a while because of where it was situated, but eventually, he found the door he needed to continue and pulled it open. He crept down the steps but wasn't prepared for what confronted him. It was just a damned furnished basement. A little dusty, but no den of evil. No, there had to be more down here.

There was another door, so he went to that, the pain he had felt upstairs was ebbing, and the feel of the woman he was following was everywhere now. Trying to hone in on her at this point was like trying to locate hay in a haystack, it was everywhere, and it all felt the same.

He almost cried when he entered the next room, a large, but simple laundry area. He couldn't understand it. While he didn't understand the weird gift God had given him either, he also knew it had never let him down before. They had to be down here damn it! But there was no more here, and there was no them!

He was almost knocked off his feet by the wave of pain that struck him. It was here, it was just hidden, it had to be here. He made his way to where the feeling was coming from, moving slowly as he tried to recover from the shock. John found himself staring like a dumbfounded idiot at a cinderblock wall. Until he saw the glint of brass near the bottom.

A moment later he could fully hear the moans of someone coming from inside the tunnel the hidden door opened to. The noise was coming from further inside, but the shape of the tunnel gave the sounds of pain an even eerie echo. John froze for a second, he had no idea what he was getting himself into here. To reassure himself he put his hand on his holster and unsnapped it. What lay ahead emanated evil like nothing in his entire life experience, this was the source of it all. That he might have to kill someone inside this place felt like a given at this point. Nobody has hidden tunnels for good reasons, and those moans didn't sound like pleasure. He had felt the pain being inflicted here, he was still feeling it wash over him, and he wanted it to end.

John forced himself to move ahead. Once the first step inside the tunnel was taken, he suddenly felt eager. The pain, the evil that had happened here was hurting him, and the only way to remove it lay ahead. He forced himself to move methodically when he wanted to bull ahead to it like a horse in the desert at an oasis. He barely registered the room the tunnel ended in, the walls lined with tools of manipulation and torture. What he needed was one door away. His patience had ended, he rushed forward and burst through.

Nothing happened at first. The occupants of the room didn't react, and he couldn't, he was too stunned by what lay in front of him. Even the sexual aspect of what he saw was beyond him and his previous life experiences. The woman he'd been following was buried up to the hilt into the other woman with a massive strap-on contraption, something that was most likely sold as a novelty since it was far too big to be enjoyable in any way. The recipient was bound to some form of table, her legs splayed wide. Her face showed an agony that had gone over to madness.

If only that was the worst of it, it would still be horrible. But instead of simple sexual perversion run amok there was far, far more. The other woman's face was mutilated beyond recognition. Her ears were missing, her hair was shorn, her eyes plucked out from her skull leaving bleeding wounds. Whatever she had looked like before was gone, leaving nothing but a mask of gore. The woman on the table moaned and tilted her head toward John as she sensed his entrance….

The spell held them all in a twisted tableau no sane artist would have painted for a moment. It couldn't last though, a second passed and the moment shattered like glass. The woman he'd come here for rudely and viciously removed the giant phallus from her victim, snarling, "Who in the fuck are you, and what in the fuck are you doing in here?"

"You!" John practically groaned as he came back to himself a bit. He rocked back on his heels as if struck before he suddenly lunged in the direction of the woman, his arms stretched out almost in supplication.

"Get the fuck away from me!" the woman growled as she swiped at his hands with her own. Pain bloomed where her hand whisked by. He hadn't seen the scalpel she had been holding, but the blood dripping from his wounded fingers attested to the fact that he had surely been its victim.

It didn't deter him, it couldn't, not now. When she swung this time, he batted her hand away and grabbed hold of her arm. In this place, touching the one who lorded over the proceedings, he had the most vibrant and clear vision of his life. He saw Carol here. Worse.

He saw the tortures this woman put his beloved sister through. The biting, the slicing; the rape by the other one became almost incidental compared to the rest.

He groaned, his soul tearing apart as he grabbed the woman with both hands and lifted her. She tried to struggle but even without the adrenaline-fueled fury he was in the grips of, she would have been no match for a man of his size. He didn't know what he was going to do until he did it. He turned completely around with the woman held above him, and then he forced her onto one of the hooks that hung from the ceiling on that side of the room.

She let out of gasp, and then with some instinct of her own she plunged the scalpel she still had in her hand into his shoulder. John stumbled back until he came into contact with the table. He didn't immediately move to remove the scalpel, as long as the steel was in place he wouldn't bleed so much. He still had things to do. Like free the poor woman strapped to the table behind him.

His good hand went to undo one of the straps, inadvertently it brushed against the deformed groaning thing. Another flash of insight hit him, insight into this woman's life.

No.

Better to burn the whole thing to the ground. He needed to get gasoline.

Patty hung where she'd been left. She had tried

reaching behind herself a couple of times to get free, only to find that there was no way on earth that was happening. She was surprised by how calm she was about the whole thing. She was in pain, breathing was incredibly difficult, she couldn't tell if it was because the hook that had slid up under her rib had pierced a lung, or if it was just the pressure of having all her weight on her ribs.

She was going to die. Even if whoever the fuck that had been didn't come back and finish the job, she'd need someone to drive her to the hospital five minutes ago to have a holy hope in hell of survival. She was going to die, right where they had tortured and killed so many. Ironic, she would be one of the very last victims. Maybe the last depending on how long the girl on the table managed to last.

She examined her mind to see what her regrets were. Other than not making sure the doors were locked, that would count as a major regret at the moment. Instead, she examined the rest of it. If she had never tracked down Bentley she wouldn't be dying right now. The thing was, in her mind, it didn't matter particularly much. She should have been happy to stay put? As if what she had been doing before that had been really living anyway. She had already been dying inside day by day before Bentley had freed her, and even now she loved him for it. No, her former life was all about being just a girl, knowing your role, sucking if you wanted to succeed. When she had learned about Bentley, she had thrown all of that out, she couldn't see herself wishing for it back just because of this.

So, she could have slowly had a lifetime of internal decay, every day a bit more until the day she was just another automaton going through the motions, or she could die today. Considering how alive she'd felt in the months with Bentley, the more she examined it, the more she was fine with today. Today was as good as any other.

Patty looked directly across the wall from herself, where the freak had written in smears of his own blood, "The Wages of Sin are Death!"

She couldn't help but chuckle, a horrible gurgling noise that hurt like hell. She managed to rasp out, "The wages of everything are death asshole, no one gets out of here alive, but not everybody lives while they're here."

Chapter 14

John thought God must be looking down on him today. Not only had he found bandages to at least stem his bleeding, but he'd also found exactly what he needed in the garage for the next part. There absolutely needed to be a next part, God himself would ask no less of him now. Large containers of diesel had appeared during his search, full to the brim just sitting there, begging to be used. He was sure if he went around the house, he'd find the generator these were meant for, but it had turned out creating light in the night wouldn't be their most important use. The light God demanded was much more important.

Cleanse it with fire in the daytime so all could see.

John hoisted the first tank with his right arm and made his slow and ponderous way to the basement. It would be more efficient to use both arms, but even with bandages the stab wound from the scalpel was oozing through. Strain it anymore and he might start bleeding so heavily that when the police showed up, he'd be lying there unconscious in a pool of fuel and blood to try and convince them as to what happened. There'd be cops eventually, but when they came, he wanted them parked by the road while the fireman tried in vain to stem the inferno.

When at last he stood in the little hallway carved through the ground he needed to take several deep breaths to work himself up to what he needed to do next. What was inside there was a bloodbath, and while some of it was his own handiwork, he certainly didn't want to look at it. Hell, he was surprised he'd managed to hold onto his lunch while he experienced it all as it happened.

Stepping back into the torture room he tried to look anywhere but at the woman dangling there or the other one strapped to the table. Which was why he finally bothered to examine the two doors across from him. When he had been in here before he had been completely tunnel visioned on that horrible woman and her victim. He tried the one to the left first and found it led to yet another set of stairs going down. He took a step down and froze. There was a soft rustling sound coming from down there. Something was moving down there!

"Go get 'em, tiger," the woman had wheezed at him with as much mockery as she could manage.

He ignored her. With his bad arm, he took his gun out and made his way down. Coming down into the room, the final chamber came into view, he could see what further terrors awaited. John almost dropped the gas can in shock. Two pale figures were crushed up against the bars of their cages expectantly, mewling nonsense words insistently. Both were naked, both of them had been identically mutated. No eyes, no ears, no nose, no hair. He almost died inside when he noticed that the woman was sporting what was almost definitely a baby bump.

The TV provided a ridiculous soundtrack of Gomer Pyle as John entered the room and began to pour fuel on anything that looked flammable. Both figures heard the splashing, but they didn't react at first. Could these things even smell anything anymore? It didn't matter, they wouldn't need to much longer.

"Have we done something wrong master? Don't you want to fuck us?" the woman asked quietly.

John had to let go of a breath ragged with emotion, but he didn't reply.

He was just leading a trail up the stairs when the TV boomed, "SURPRISE! SURPRISE! SURPRISE!"

Nothing shocked him anymore, when he went to the last room and saw that there were the beginnings of a new bone pile there, he felt nothing. Just hit it with fuel and move on, that was the way of it. He moved by both women, noting they still lived and just dribbled fuel as he went splashing some on both, eliciting dull groans They were just two Halloween decorations whose batteries were running out. Upstairs he even unplugged the refrigerator and the full freezer, opened the doors to both and splashed fuel inside. He was in a frenzy, everything needed to be cleansed by fire. He didn't so much as dare allow himself to think about the meat inside that freezer, he had more than enough for all his future nightmares.

He was back in the garage when he realized he didn't have a lighter.

The whole house was set to go up like a tinderbox and he didn't have the spark.

In a panic he began to rip apart the garage shelves, throwing more flammable material on the ground as he knocked over container after container of paint thinners and the like. Something in here had to provide the flame. Something in here burned. Why have the fuel without the fire?

He forced himself to step outside and calm down. He needed to think, not just create a racket like a lunatic getting himself woozy on the fumes. John took great gulping breaths of fresh air when he reached outdoors hoping that if breathed deeply enough the horror would be expelled from his lungs so he wouldn't carry that taint inside him forever. His face turned upward toward the sun as if just the warming rays of it could rinse the vileness that had soaked into his pores inside this den of murder and torture.

He opened his eyes and saw the grill sitting on the patio.

Fifteen minutes later he could see the rising flames in the distance as he was driving away.

Hare picked up his phone on the second ring.

"Hare here."

"Detective, I know who your killer is," came a familiar voice.

"What? Who is this.... wait is this, John?" Hare sputtered.

"Detective, I don't have a lot of time. I need any alternative address you have on file or a workplace for whoever lives at 2021 Sycamore Lane."

"How can, you be sure?"

"Detective, I was inside, please, we may not have much time," John replied heatedly.

Hare tried to form coherent thoughts, fingers flying over the keyboard. Finally, he managed to spit out, "Look, we have that address, why on earth would we need anything else?"

"I don't think he's going to go back there, just please look it up."

Hare was too flustered to argue, he flipped through his computer to public records and ran it up automatically. He wasn't supposed to do things like that, but John had got to him with this. John's track record combined with his tone of voice told Hare to follow through. There were long silent moments, broken only by John's breathing on the phone before he returned. "I got a Bentley Thomas. You were right, it looks like he has another place in the mountains, about an hour or two from there. Address is 201 Huckleberry Lane if you can believe that. I checked it on Google, it's a cabin or something. Look just hold tight and I'll head up there and let you know what we find. I can have my partner check his place of work."

"Detective, I am heading up there right now. I told you; I NEED to be there when he's apprehended. I gave you your serial killer, now you need to do your part and give me mine," John said calmly.

"Look, just...just don't go up there alone. We've got a better chance if we both went up. Hell, we'd have a better chance if we sent a swat team, but if you're heading up right now anyway at least.... Look, can we meet up somewhere and go up together?" Hare asked.

"Certainly, in fact, I'd be rather obliged if you brought a first aid kit, and a needle and thread. I'm a bit cut up," John said.

"Are you sure you don't want to put this off?"

"No, I'm sure he'll run if we don't get him now. As in right now, not as soon as you can get a team, not when I have a chance to heal up, like right now."

Hare paused for a moment before he said, "How do you know that?"

"I'm afraid I might have tipped him off when I burnt his house down."

There was a lengthy pause before Hare said, "All right, let me text you the address of a convenience store near where we're going, we can meet there."

Hare pulled up and saw John's truck immediately, Thankfully the man was inside it, at this point he hadn't been sure if the guy might still try to go it alone. Hare hated that he'd promised this guy anything right now while secretly admitting they wouldn't have a damned thing if he hadn't. He also wished he could have called a SWAT team in to apprehend the killer John swore awaited them. Especially after what had happened the last time someone had gone solo to apprehend somebody suspected of being a serial killer around here. The problem was, he didn't even have an actual active murder investigation here to call anyone in on. It was why he hadn't told Burke; Burke was basking in the glow of the face stealer case being wrapped, he refused to believe there was a second serial killer wandering around when they already had one in the morgue. Any probable cause would be waiting until the fire department put out the guy's house. And John was right about one thing, if the guy had any sense whatsoever, he'd be long gone by then.

Hare got a good look at his psychic when the man opened his door. The man looked pale and worn out. Hare called out, "Not here, most of these places have exterior cameras, and me patching you up in the parking lot would count as evidence. Follow me, there's a park nearby. But if you don't think you're bleeding to death at the moment, I want a coffee."

Hare had also bought a bottle of alcohol which he was rinsing John's cuts out with before he stitched them up. It was frankly almost a relief to see the man's stoic veneer crack a little when the liquid splashed onto the gashes. It proved the guy was human after all. Working with someone like this could put doubts in your head, he was physically imposing to go with a set of abilities you couldn't even comprehend. Add in the quiet and self-effacing demeanor and it was enough to make you scared of the guy. Considering what he had said he'd just done; it would appear that fear was completely justified.

Hare had finished threading the needle and was making a start on the stitches that absolutely had to happen when he finally asked, "Care to tell me why in the fuck you burnt down his house? You know, the place with all the evidence?"

"Had to," John grunted as Hare pulled the thread through.

Hare grunted back as he started the next stitch, "You would be surprised at how often I don't have to burn something to the ground. In fact, other than a wasp's nest, I don't think it's ever come up. So, any reason why you had to burn this place down?"

John sighed, "I have never been in a single place as evil as that. I mean, not just psychically, I wouldn't try to feed you that, if I didn't get results you wouldn't believe that crap existed. I mean what happened there, the evidence, some of it will probably survive… Look…. People didn't just get killed there, they were tortured for a long time, they were violated, and then their bones were stored in an empty room in a sub-basement like keepsakes. It just...God's earth is a better place for the flames. When this is all over, I may go over there with salt for the earth."

Now it was Hare's turn to sigh, "Well, my earth would be a whole lot better with the evidence that is currently being reduced to ash, that's all I can say."

Bentley was just about packed and not a moment too soon. It was time to go. He was worried. Patty wasn't answering and one of the neighbors had just called to say his house was engulfed in flames. He couldn't afford to view any of that as coincidence It didn't sound like the cops had made him yet, except for Waco they usually don't just burn the place down.... but someone had. He could keep trying Patty from the road, but he would have to assume she'd been in there. Even if her phone had been and she hadn't she'd have found a way to call. If she was alive, he could send for her, but something had gone south, Bentley just didn't know what it was yet. If she wasn't alive, he'd mourn her, and find a way to make whoever did it die in ways not heard of since the fucking dark ages. But to do that he had to create room to think.

He froze as he closed the last suitcase. He heard tires on stones down the hill from the house. Somebody was especially clever; they knew about the cabin and had come to talk to him about what they knew, he was sure of it. He picked up his rifle which he'd planned to be the last thing in the SUV and turned the scope down through the trees to the base of his drive. Well, that made it weird, a cop, but right behind him was a big old redneck pickup. This did not look like an official business, the fire hadn't been either. It looked like someone had gone off the reservation to get Bentley.

They parked just past the base of the driveway, where you wouldn't notice them if it wasn't for the scope he was looking through. Doors opened and two men got out, one was definitely police material, but the other... He pinned the scope on the guy's face, there was something in those eyes. The cop might have plans to arrest Bentley, but somehow, he didn't think that was the other guy's hope for how all this was going to play out.

Bentley waited as the men tried to skulk their way up to the cabin by keeping to the woods. Yeah, one cop, and one hillbilly sneaking up was definitely not police procedure, especially after what just happened to that fed at their copycat's house. The cops should be on strict by the book rules after something like that. So, somebody with a friend on the force had figured it out and had come calling. All righty then. It wasn't like Bentley was planning on staying here, or even staying Bentley after the calls he'd made during the last day. He could afford one more bloodbath. Patty, and all that he had left of his mother demanded one.

He sighted carefully and pulled the trigger.

There was a cloud of red that blossomed from Hare's hip as the slug shattered the bone. The man dropped like a rock clutching at himself and screaming in pain. One down…

Instead of helping his friend, the other man just put up his hands and started walking up the road, right up toward the cabin. Bentley could easily drop him, but he had to admit, he was curious. This was a damned ballsy move on the guy's part, he had to know Bentley had him dead to rights. This was almost the move of a real honest-to-God human being, and Bentley didn't kill those if he didn't have to.

When the man was close enough, he bellowed into the air at the top of his lungs, "Bentley! You're obviously in there! Look, I know what you've done. All of it. You killed my sister; I want to talk about it!"

Very ballsy indeed.

Well, might as well play this last drama out. He could always shoot the guy if he didn't like the way it was going. Bentley looked down and saw the military knife he'd been planning to pack into the car sitting on the nightstand. He decided that skin removal might be in the future, so he pocketed it. Bentley walked to the front door and opened it, standing in the shadows of the darkened cabin, barely visible from outside. But there was no mistaking the glint of the gun in his hand.

"All right, so let's hear what you have to say, you got me curious," Bentley called out through the door.

"I know you killed my sister because I killed the woman who helped you," the man said more quietly now that he didn't have to yell so much.

A part of Bentley died inside, murdered with a sudden stab of pain right to his chest. Somehow, he maintained his composure and nodded, "So I'm looking at the firestarter. Guess that means you killed my pets down in the basement too. Don't that make us just about even?"

"No" the man replied flatly.

"That would be strictly a matter of opinion. I was very fond of Patty, and my babies down in the basement never did a damned thing to you. What's your name buddy? I like your spunk and everything, so before I shoot you, I'd like to know the name of the guy I put down."

"It's John. But I figure you won't shoot me, not when you can beat my ass for killing your lady love. Call it a pride thing, and I figure you have a lot of that to go around, am I right?"

Bentley chuckled, "Or, I could just shoot you."

John nodded, "You could do that, but then you wouldn't have had that last chance to really hurt me for what I did. To whup the man who came here for revenge, the man who killed your woman. You wouldn't get that, would you? I mean look at me, you can see the blood on me, it isn't all someone else's"

"And why in the hell would you even risk it, if you're so damned unsure about winning?"

"I just want to put my fist in the face of the man who killed the only woman I love before I die."

There was a long, quiet moment that hung there, punctuated only by the occasional moan from Hare a bit further down the road. Finally, Bentley said, "Well, that piece in your holster is going to have to fuck right off before I even take my bead off your head."

"Fair enough," John said before he unstrapped the holster. He held it up for Bentley to see, and then threw it hard behind him so it landed past where Hare lay.

"Your buddy's pieces too, he'll have his shoulder harness, but he'll also have a throw-down either in the small of his back or on his ankle, both of them can go make friends with your gun."

John nodded before walking back to the fallen detective.

"What in the hell are you doing?" Hare hissed between clenched teeth, his eyes barely open from the pain.

"I'm going to kick his ass," John said matter-of-factly as he slapped the detective's hands away and unbuckled Hare's shoulder harness. Hare couldn't reach down that far to prevent him from finding the promised throw-down weapon.

"If you don't, we're fucked," Hare managed.

John threw the two weapons lightly where they landed near his own gun. "Yeah, considering he's got a bead on my head, we're already currently pretty fucked as is, so SNAFU all around." Turning back, he yelled to Bentley, "Satisfied?"

"Well, if that's the way you want it," Bentley said as he set down his rifle. The truth was, as bad as this guy wanted to beat his ass, Bentley wanted to hurt him just as bad. Patty had been the first time since his mother that he'd felt love towards anyone, and this bastard just admitted that he'd killed her. All that was left of his mother, the woman who had taught him how to be human had been in that house, the house this fucker admitted to burning down. If he wanted a fight, Bentley was up for it. Bentley didn't have a bloody shoulder for one thing, or tape wrapping the fingers of one hand. He assumed those were parting kisses from his beloved. He wanted to feel her one more time, even if it meant biting those damned fingers off.

The second Bentley stepped down from the porch John charged at him, arms outstretched to tackle him. Bentley moved quicker than John anticipated and even managed to throw a glancing blow that caught John on the jaw as he went by in a cloud of dust.

His own momentum and the force of the punch disoriented John for a moment, he lost track of the other man. When he learned where Bentley was, it was because Bentley had just thrown a vicious kick into

John's back that threw the man to the ground, the top of his head bouncing off the bottom step. John felt a tug from the stitches, but thankfully, so far, they were holding.

Bentley was grinning viciously as he moved forward to inflict more pain on his opponent. He was just winding his foot up when suddenly John's foot lashed out in a sweeping motion that caught Bentley's plant leg and sent Bentley tumbling forward, where John's other boot thrust up and caught him in the solar plexus.

Bentley stumbled away from John gagging and wheezing as he tried to get his breath back from the blow. John crawled slowly to his own feet his vision blurry from the blow to the head. Seeing Bentley still not recovered he made another stumbling lunge at his opponent. Unlike the previous time, Bentley couldn't dart away, but John was still not coherent enough to take advantage. Instead, both men tumbled down the drive in the direction of Hare.

The fall had sent both men a little apart from one another. As they struggled to their feet, Bentley grinned a bit. Fresh blood had bloomed on John's shirt. Crimson proof his girl had gotten some shots in before she died. Good for her. Now he just needed to drop this SOB to make him really suffer for what he did.

Bentley threw another punch as soon as he got to his feet. John hadn't even been looking at him, but somehow, he managed to block it and throw a crashing blow of his own with his good arm. It cracked right into Bentley's jaw clean, sending the man hurtling backward. There was a brutal thump when Bentley's head hit the ground, and he lay there still.

John stumbled over to him, feeling the blood flowing freely from his shoulder, and now his hands as well. All of Hare's stitches had been blown, and the wounds were flowing free and clear. It didn't matter, the bastard was down. John would be able to finish this. No macho screwing around, no poses, no speeches, it was time for all this horror to end.

He straddled Bentley's prone form. His thumbs reached out and found Bentley's windpipe.

Hare groaned from where he lay, "Don't do it John, let me take him in."

A riot of emotions flooded through John. He could kill this vile thing right now. It would be so damned easy. Then he considered, how had this all started? When had he put his foot on the path that had led him to where he was now? He had handled vengeance for himself before. He might have said it was for Carol, but it hadn't made her feel any better, only himself. And what was the result of his pride? Carol dead, him about to commit murder right in front of a cop. He considered Bentley's arrogance and weighed it against his own.

In a rasping voice, he said, "You're right, better he dies in prison like a dog. A whipped cur with no power over anyone ever again."

He began to climb to his feet.

Which was when Bentley lunged upward and forward with the knife he'd had stashed in his pocket, "just in case."

The thrust couldn't have been any truer. John felt his strength drain away in an instant as the blade plunged through the springy wall of skin, through the meat of a hardworking man, and directly into his kidney. Bentley pulled it out and a rush of crimson flowed down John's shirt and began to stain his jeans.

John knew he was dying and dying rapidly. He used the moment to assess himself one last time and was horrified by what he saw. He saw a man who had used his gifts to allow himself to be brought low. He could have, at every step of the way, allowed justice to take its course. At every step, the night Carol came home bruised and crying until now, he had allowed himself to sink to the level of those he hated. Vengeance comes from the lord, justice comes from the law, misery was all that came at his hands. And now those hands had been made weak and useless. Justice belonged to the Lord because redemption and repentance belonged to him, John had closed that road for others and had brought the Lord's wrath down upon himself.

Bentley kicked out, and the big man went over like a felled tree landing face down.

The woods were quiet for a moment.

Hare heard Bentley before he saw him. He looked up in terror as the killer loomed over him. He should have called Burke; he should have taken John into protective custody…. And that was just today, a lifetime of regrets paraded across the screen of his mind for what was sure to be his last moments on earth.

Bentley smiled.

"Now, you could die here. You very well could. It is all up to you detective, and I'm figuring you for a detective. Or let's try a story out. You heard the man confess to killing three people and burning my house down. You were trailing a suspected murderer who was obsessed with me for some reason. I wasn't here at this home either, and a fight broke out between the two of you, he shot you, and when he was coming to finish the deed, you stabbed him, fatally. Let's consider that option, why don't we? Now that is a lovely story that gets rid of a lot of complications, for me, and for you. Or I could just leave you right here and let you bleed out. Trust me, once you turn up the road you've got service, inside your car you could call dispatch, you could live. Hell, I could make sure you died by just waiting you out a bit. It would still look the same really. Those rooms in my house were rigged, by the way, I promise you, you won't find an ounce of evidence to tie me to anything no matter how big a shovel you bring."

"Why would you let me live?" Hare gasped.

"I'm a nice guy," Bentley said. Seeing Hare's face he

started laughing, "No, I'm just fucking with you. I'm leaving, there's not a damned thing keeping me here anymore. My girl is dead, all of my family keepsakes have burned in the fire, I got no good reason to stay here, and lots of great ones to leave. I'm going to say publicly that after this crazed stalker, I don't feel safe here anymore.

But there's more, you enabled this fucker, you encouraged this psycho. And trust me, the guy was nuttier than a Payday. Hear him talking 'bout the only woman he ever loved? That the kind of legacy you want to protect Mr. Policeman? And I want to get a little of mine on you for this mess. When I'm gone, I want you to always have this to think about. You are never going to know exactly what happened here. I'm willing to bet it will be the reason for your future drinking problem. Not to mention, I suspect you might be an honest-to-God person deep down, and I don't like killing people."

"What choice have I got?" Hare gasped.

"Not a fucking one if you want to live. And of course, if you go back on your end of this, I can always hunt you down later. I'm good at that shit. I am going to leave that little statement that makes you look like a hero with my lawyer, but good luck finding anyone named Bentley Thomas next week."

"Since I've got no choice, I guess I'm doing it, but I just want to say, fuck you," Hare growled.

"I ain't got the time to pop your cherry today son.

Just be glad it wasn't worse. It could ALWAYS be worse, remember that," Bentley said as he got back to his feet and began walking toward the cabin.

The sun had begun its graceful descent over the mountains when Bentley's SUV reached the main road and rode off into the early evening. Hare heard it go from where Bentley had helped him into his own car. He turned on the radio and called dispatch.

Epilogue

The sun was setting over the desert, it made for the prettiest time of the day. A time to stare off at the distant mountains and consider the world. He thought about whether he'd ever find another girl like Patty. Somehow, he doubted it, that girl was one of a kind. She had more than depths to her, she'd had chasms he could get lost in and forget himself. He had girlfriends but he kept them at arm's length. People were special, they couldn't just be replaced, only drones carried that luxury. Still, where there's life there's hope. He needed to believe that there would be someone out there for him, someone human to share his world.

In the meantime, Bentley had a good life. A nice house that used to belong to a drug lord, a new job, and a new hunting ground. The drug lord hadn't known he was going to happily sell to Bentley. Drones can be monsters, but it took a real human being to cause horror beyond imagining.

Bentley would have a great life down here if only he had her to share it with. Gruesome crimes and disappearances got blamed on the cartels down here on the border. But the nice thing was, the face of a Spanish-speaking drone came off just as easily as the ones back home. Screams were the universal language.

Author's Note:

Wow! Are you reading this? Nobody reads the author's notes, they just rush off to Goodreads to put another notch into their yearly challenge. Good for you though, I appreciate you.

Well, that was a mess, huh? I mean, I hope you saw that I was aiming at more than just blood everywhere, but if you didn't, I hope you enjoyed it. For everyone who's done guessing what in the hell I was aiming for exactly, let me explain a bit since I doubt any English Lit course is going to want to discuss it. Might as well get it all out in the open.

First thing, the main gist of it really, is how we view our fellow man. We categorize, we box up, we label, and we remove their humanity so we can feel justified in our opinions. Dehumanizing our perceived enemies is how we justify our atrocities. If someone is no longer human, then it doesn't matter what we do to them. It is our empathy for each other that prevents us from being monsters.

I also wanted the reader to feel like they were rooting for Bentley and Patty, even if they didn't realize it until it was too late. Call it me poking fun at all our love for a good anti-hero. I include myself here. Ezra was far worse than they were, John wrapped himself up in morality but ended up flawed through and through…. You were kinda' stuck with them.

As far as the over-the-top amount of sex. I wanted it that way to remove the titillation of it. Just to be so relentless that nobody in their right mind could get off on it. Of course, since this is Splatterpunk, someone will accuse all of us of getting off on it. Fuck 'em. Or don't, make sure you have consent first and play safe and all that, the safe word is pumpernickel. Whatever you do past that is between the two of you, I don't kink shame.

There's more, but you can debate it amongst yourselves. And if you hate read this just so you can slam it later as being sick and depraved, why don't you go the fuck outside and get a goddamned hobby or something? Geez, life's too short.

Hope you had fun and got thoughtful about the chaos.

P.J.

FROM ST ROOSTER BOOKS

From Tim Murr

The Gray Man
978-1799252177
Motel on Fire; Stories
978-1543039016
Neon Sabbath; Stories

978-1721039708
My Skull is Full of Black Smoke: Stories
979-8680276099
Thirsty and Miserable: A Critical Analysis of the Music of Black Flag
979-8609363220
Texas is the Reason: Five Decades of the Texas Chainsaw Massacre
979-8374744392
Summer's Venomous Kiss
979-8378167012
Whatever Happened to Spiderbaby Jane? b/w Snake Eater
979-8860069916

Collection/Various Authors

To Be One with You: An Anthology of Parasitic Horror 2018 featuring Paul Kane, Marie O'Regan, Jeffery X Martin, Peter Oliver Wonder, Adam Millard, DJ Tyrer, David W Barbee, Ross Peterson
978-1724516787
Kids of the Black Hole; A Punksploitation Anthology featuring Sarah Miner, Chris Hallock, Paul Lubaczewski, and Jeremy Lowe
978-1072962724
The Blind Dead Ride Out of Hell; A Literary Tribute to the Amando de Ossorio Films featuring Sam Richard, Heather

Drain, Paul Lubaczewski, Mark Zirbel, Jeremy Lowe, and
Jerome Reuter

979-8692365187

A New Life by Paul Lubaczewski

979-8615384066

Blood & Mud by John Baltisberger

The God Provides by Thomas R Clark

979-8520227076

3 Hits from the Holler by Paul Lubaczewski

979-8707581984

Abhorrent Siren by John Baltisberger

978-1955745024

Let the World Drown: An Anthology of Sea Horror
featuring Brian M Sammons, Lee Franklin, Jedediah Smith,
AK McCarthy, Anthony S Buoni, BE Goose, Paul
Lubaczewski, Jeremy Lowe, John Baltisberger, and Carter
Johnson

979-8739852915

Souls in a Blender by Lamont A Turner

979-8494735201

Hungry Cosmos by Reed Alexander

979-8776862472

Black Friday: An Elder's Keep Collection by Jeffery X
Martin

978-1955745093

Abhorrent Faith by John Baltisberger

978-1955745093

Short Stories About You by Jeffery X Martin

9798438145318

I Never Eat…Cheesesteak by Paul Lubaczewski

979-8440821415

Hunting Witches by Jeffery X Martin

979-8832793955

Saint's Blood by Ryan C Bradley

979-8804031863

As the Night Devours Us by Villimey Mist
979-8834327097
Parham's Field by Jeffery X Martin
SummerHome by Thomas R Clark
979-8838185136
The Ridge by Jeffery X Martin
979-8354516568
Through the Mist and the Madness: An Analytical Thesis on the First Three Metallica Albums by Jerome Reuter
979-8354143696
Like a Ton of Bricks by Paul Lubaczewski
979-8367912081
The Flock by Jeffery X Martin
979-8365780941
A Prayer from the Dead by Thomas R Clark
979-8393890742
Wax Figures by Aaron Weese
979-8390704202
Razor Blade in the Fun-Size Candy: A Horror Comedy Anthology edited by Paul Lubaczewski featuring Jeff Strand, John Wayne Communale, Bridgette Nelson, Robert Essig, Tony Evans, John Baltisberger, Mikki Nelson-Hicks, RJ Bennetti, Christine Morgan, Damien Casey, Kyra R Torres, Kenzie Jennings, Michael Allen Rose, Nikolas P Robinson
979-8395371195
Bleeding Out in the Rain by Lamont A Turner
979-8852235145
Brooklyn Hardcore by Eddie MacNamara
979-8850638979
Even More Monsters by Paul Kane
979-8859240890
Electric Funeral: Black Sabbath and the Cultural Landscape 1970-1975 by Jerome Reuter
979-8854150477
Droplets: Stories by Paul Lubaczewski

9798879721935
Under a Starless Sky by Lamont A Turner
979-8324229252

304